THE FLY-TRUFFLER

THE FLY-TRUFFLER

Gustaf Sobin

BLOOMSBURY

First published 1999

Copyright © 1999 by Gustaf Sobin

The moral right of the author has been asserted

Bloomsbury Publishing Plc, 38 Soho Square, London WIV 5DF

A CIP catalogue record for this book
is available from the British Library

ISBN 0 7475 4466 2

10 9 8 7 6 5 4 3 2 1

Typeset in Great Britain by Hewer Text Ltd, Edinburgh
Printed in Great Britain by Clays Ltd, St Ives plc

I

He'd take the same path, now, nearly every morning. Following the edge of the oak woods, he'd tap the undergrowth as he came with a curious little branch he'd whittled for the very occasion. The branch itself had been stripped of everything but a narrow wedge of pine needles at its extremity. Tapping, patting the undergrowth, he could easily have been mistaken for a blind man. Yes, a blind man or – seen from a certain distance – someone with a metal detector scrutinizing the ground in search of some small archeological treasure. Philippe Cabassac, however, was neither blind nor in search of treasure. Tall, heavyset, his entire frame seemed concentrated within the cone of his gaze, and his gaze – fixed, obsessive – upon the surface of the ground before him.

'Come on,' he murmured to the ground itself, 'let's see your wings, your little wings.' His murmur, barely perceptible, was hardly more than the abrasion of one dry lip against another. 'Come on,' he insisted, using what he called the old language – that now nearly extinct idiom – in addressing *lei mousco*, the flies. For he was begging the flies for a sign: some tiny, covert, telltale indication.

With the oak woods on one side, the abandoned almond orchards on the other, Cabassac held the sun fixed like a compass point directly before him. That way, he knew, he wouldn't be casting a shadow over the brittle winter grasses: the very haunt of those tiny, strawlike insects. Wouldn't be disturbing those diptera until the very last second. Because it was their sudden, spasmodic flight that betrayed their secret. They'd spring rather than fly, revealing as they did the exact point over which they'd just perched. It was there, in the heavily scented earth directly beneath, that they'd lay their eggs. There, too, but at a depth of ten, twenty, even thirty centimeters, that – by a miracle of pure symbiosis – one of those black, odoriferous tubers could be found. One of those coveted truffles, firmly cradled in the very earth it so richly embalmed.

'Come on,' he went on muttering as much to himself as to any one of those evanescent insects. For the fly, the truffle that the fly invariably unmasked, and Cabassac's own most personal fantasies had become perfectly contiguous. Over the past few months, the three had come to constitute in his mind the trinity of a single, inseparable association.

Gently beating the grasses with that little whisk broom he'd whittled out of a pine branch, Cabassac scrutinized the patch of earth before him. Magnified by the heavy, steel-rimmed spectacles that he wore, the wrinkles at the corner of his eyes had narrowed to a grimace. It was as if all the grief he'd borne over the past two years – profound but inexpressible – could at last come to focus. Could linger, just then, on a patch of tall, bristling lavender or crouch to a spread of that all-auspicious pink perennial – the stonecrop – hoping to dislodge therein one of those thin, strawlike insects. They'd spring, each time, like sparks, flying at random off the flat, battered horns of some black anvil. Like keys, too, he thought. Like tiny, golden keys. *Claus d'aur*, as he put it in that nearly extinct idiom of his. For the flies, properly observed, not only revealed where a buried truffle lay but, so doing, inaugurated – he'd recently discovered – a whole, hallucinatory under-world unto itself.

It had taken Cabassac a considerable amount of time to discover this fact. Like any Provençal living in an area of loose, calcareous topsoil, he'd truffled – fly-truffled – ever since childhood. In his family, the truffle was considered a delicacy, a seasonal treat. It was, in fact, a recurrent part of one's winter diet, diced into gener-ous black slices, then either mixed in a salad of crisp, curly-headed lettuce or fried – but scarcely – into an omelette. The truffle was never fully cooked (a heresy in the world of trufflers, for cooking markedly reduced the aroma) nor conserved. It was consumed fresh from mid-November until early March and then, if not forgotten, relegated to that natural calendar in which the earth alone determined the sequence of events. Philippe Cabassac, approaching fifty, had basked in its delicate aroma every winter of his life. It had accompanied him through his childhood, his years at the university as student, research scholar, and professor, and – until recently – through his brief, belated, yet boundlessly happy marriage. Never, though, had it taken on the properties that it had since his wife's death. Never before had the fly been considered a 'golden key' and the truffle – that obscure cryptogam – an agent of epiphanous visions.

It had taken Cabassac quite some time to realize this. An ardent rationalist, a man steeped in the philosophy of the Provençal Enlightenment, he'd waited two full years before admitting that the truffle – the consumption of the truffle – had begun affecting his dreams. Was bringing him, each time, closer and closer to the beloved figure of his wife, Julieta.

'Come on,' he pleaded, 'give me a sign. A quick little flicker.' Stooping low over a thick cluster of brome-grass, he murmured as a pilgrim might before some sacred relic. Well over two hundred pounds and solidly built, Cabassac brought his entire mass to bear in scrutinizing each and every blade. At any given instant, one of those *claus d'aur*, the little keys to that oneiric underworld he'd only recently come to discover, could easily break free.

Cabassac knew that the truffle wasn't some kind of hallucinogenic. It didn't belong, he realized, to the pharmacopoeia of dreams: to those potions, elixirs, that operated so faultlessly on the neurons of the dreaming mind. The power of the truffle resided in something far more subtle, refined. Indeed, it had no direct effect on one's dream life whatsoever. To the contrary, the truffle affected one's awakened body, one's conscious thoughts. It reassured the senses with its warm, earthly aroma, placed one's entire being in a raised state of receptivity. It didn't provoke the dream so much as create the conditions – the *dispousicioun*, as Cabassac put it – in which the dream might occur. Consumed, assimilated, the truffle would leave him feeling perfectly disposed to receive whatever rich, flickering images those dreams had to offer.

The first year after Julieta's death, he only dreamt of her in pieces: a shoulder; a huge, lustrous eye floating over a bed of flowers; the shaft of her thighs like some shattered bit of statuary. It was as if death had left her decimated in so many hopelessly disparate, ephemeral sections. Even her whispers, that first year, reached Cabassac in a succession of scattered fragments. Words, occasional phrases, the truncated segments of what might have been some promissory message, reached him like spume bursting over the walls of some invisible breakwater. Reached him, too, like the rare, scarcely legible passages of an otherwise obliterated antique text. Immersed in such a state, he cherished every syllable. Tried to recall each and every broken utterance upon awakening. Would even scribble whatever he remembered on a notepad he kept alongside his bed for that very purpose. Of all her utterances, though, the one which repeated most often was 'why.' A 'why' without object, without subject: a great, gaping, irrecusable 'why.' Philippe Cabassac received the immense implications of that tiny word particle as something bequeathed: something that Julieta had entrusted him with. Why, she could only be asking, was she on one side of that impenetrable curtain and he on the other? It was a question he felt called upon to answer.

The winter of that first year of widowerhood, Cabassac hadn't yet equated truffles with dreams: the consummation of those mysterious tubers with their ensuing revelations. Perhaps, too, in all the turbulence of that first year, there was no equation to be made. He'd go out truffling as he had since childhood. He did so more out of habit, as a means of passing time each weekend, than for the sake of satisfying some particular purpose. Listlessly, he'd comb the very edge of those abandoned almond orchards, tapping the grasses dryly, mechanically, as he went. Nothing mattered that first year. Nothing moved him if not those brief, electrifying moments in which his wife – his Julieta – appeared, no matter how piecemeal, in so many dream apparitions. He lived for those moments. Each day, all day, he'd bide his time, waiting for the night in which – quick, brilliant, self-extinguishing as some meteor trail – he might catch glimpses of that cherished being.

Come spring, those moments grew scarcer. Cabassac had no way of knowing, of course, that the scarcity of his dreams, now, coincided with the end of the truffle season. He hadn't yet made that mysterious equation between one buried thing and another: between the tuber, nestled in its damp soil, and his beloved, laid to rest in an earthen chamber of her own. Hadn't yet drawn a line between the evocative powers of the one and the dazzling evocations of the other.

That first year, Cabassac lived like a kind of automaton. He went through the motions, each morning, of dressing, preparing his own breakfast, driving forty kilometers into Avignon three times a week to teach his advanced studies course in Provençal linguistics. He scarcely noticed how the enrollment in that class, already low and limited – furthermore – to a select group of graduate students, had gone on diminishing. Given that he lectured in an auditorium that normally seated two hundred, the number of students that remained, scattered throughout, served as a sullen reminder of that vanishing world. The study of Provençal had lost its hold over the past few decades. It had become, finally, a rarefied pursuit for a privileged few. Cabassac's arrival on the Avignon faculty, however, had at first resuscitated interest in that dying language, that wilting discipline. He'd brought water to its roots, light to the very tip of its branches. His lectures were reputed to be luminous, captivating, memorable. Those who attended, however few, invariably fell under his spell, and found his commitment to the preservation of that vanishing *lengage* thoroughly contagious.

Since Julieta's death, however, Cabassac had lost all passion for teaching. He read his lectures off a sheaf of hastily scribbled notes, now, mumbling them mechanically, hardly looking up to meet the gaze of his students throughout that nearly deserted auditorium. They, in turn, grew scarcer. One by one, they began dropping out. And those who remained did so more out of academic obligation than any deep-seated intellectual curiosity. They'd fidget through his lackluster deliveries or stare, dreamily, at the leaves of a paulownia lapping at a skylight overhead. None took notes, now, as they had only months earlier. Cabassac's once crystalline remarks on, say, some seemingly minor, syntactical trait, containing the germ of a major cultural characteristic (the rootedness of most Provençal nouns, for instance, at the expense of inference, abstraction), had all but vanished.

Cabassac merely went through the motions. He still pretended – as best as he could – to teach, shared meals from time to time with a colleague or some remnant of his family, and dealt – like everyone else – with that unending succession of chores, commitments, responsibilities that life, unendingly, generates. Not the least of those responsibilities concerned the sale, each year, of some parcel of Cabassac's property. Pressed by debts over the past decade, he was repeatedly obliged to sell off an abandoned terrace, a fallow wheat field or several acres of virgin oak grove. He had no other way of making ends meet. His salary as part-time professor in a highly discredited department didn't begin to cover Cabassac's expenditures, low as they were. Despite his spartan life, he still had to pay property taxes on that vast, sprawling estate he'd inherited as well as meet an endless array of food, fuel and electricity bills. Even if his personal needs were minimal and his follies non-existent, he found himself dialing – come year's end – the local real estate agent, and offering up yet another parcel of his ever-diminishing estate.

'Well, what's it going to be this year,' the realtor asked, 'orchards or vineyards? Or just another spread of good old oak wood?' Cold, jovial, perfunctory, he'd put Cabassac through the same tasteless ritual each winter. From the very first, the realtor had wanted to buy his entire estate outright, including the great, ramshackle farmhouse Cabassac had always inhabited, as had at least eight generations of ancestors. For several years running the realtor had made every possible offer, exerted every possible pressure. But Cabassac had resisted. He'd sell off exactly what he needed each year to meet expenses but not a square centimeter more. For Cabassac, the farm, the fields, the woods – handed down through all those generations of peasant ancestry – constituted a kind of living organism. Selling off even the smallest parcel suggested an act of severance, amputation. It filled Cabassac with a profound sense of betrayal. The property had been not only his legacy but his nursery, his hedge school, his personal universe for the better part of his life. Even the wildest, most worthless patch of undergrowth – rich with berries and birds' eggs – had deeply colored the psychic geography of his very existence.

Cabassac not only felt remorseful in selling off bits of his property each year, but puzzled. He often wondered why the realtor hadn't resold those very plots. Why, for instance, had none of it already passed into the hands of third parties either for the sake of house construction or for some form of agricultural recycling? What was the real estate agent waiting for? For every last abandoned terrace? Every collapsed retaining wall? For the shell of each and every outlying dependency? What else could the realtor possibly be waiting for, he often thought, but everything?

Cabassac, nonetheless, went on truffling each winter just as he went on gathering wild asparagus each spring, flowering medicinal herbs each summer, and a plethora of pale, speckled mushrooms each fall. It was all part of Cabassac's natural calendar. Nothing could have kept him from observing that cycle in all its aspects and manifestations. Even now, entering the second year of his widowerhood, dumb to virtually everything that surrounded him, Cabassac took to the woods. Dumb even to the woods themselves and to that massive shadow he hauled across their undergrowth, even to his own heart at the very heart of that shadow, he felt magnetized, nonetheless, to that cycle: that seasonal ritual he observed simply because he could not have done otherwise.

Driven by instinct, by a set of hidden tropistic signals, Cabassac went on tapping at the tall gaunt plumage of lavender, ferreting through so many flat, ground-hugging mats of stonecrop with that whisk broom he'd whittled for the very occasion. Come that second winter, Cabassac flushed one evanescent fly after another from its haunt, and the truffle it invariably betrayed. Indeed, it was a prolific year for that mysterious tuber. Cabassac, however, only unearthed what he needed for his own immediate purposes. With a slightly curved iron bar, he'd uproot two or three of those dense, black, globular nuggets, never smaller than a walnut and sometimes every bit as large as a crab apple. Still, for Cabassac, the truffle was nothing more than a winter condiment, a deeply appreciated, wonderfully pungent, seasonal additive. It hadn't yet acquired, that is, its secondary characteristics.

But in that second winter after Julieta's death, Cabassac came at last to make the association: between the ingestion of the truffle and the increasingly evocative dreams he'd begun having of his wife. One night in late December, he felt an especially heightened state of well-being after having consumed a particularly odoriferous truffle. This rare – and most welcome – condition seemed to affect his general state of mind as never before. By January, he'd come to realize that this very state had extended into his dream life: that his dreams were becoming more and more vivid. More and more protracted. One night, after having had an especially succulent truffle omelette, he'd even dreamt that the two of them made love. Slowly, languorously, without

14

the least trace of precipitation, they'd moved for hours, it seemed, cradled by a rhythm as telluric as it was corporal. Like some kind of mild earthen pulsation, that rhythm beat – syncretic – through their very bodies. Throbbed, unabated, through the furthest reaches of their being. During that entire dream sequence, Julieta had kept her head turned to one side, her gaze fixed upon the far wall. Dark, immense, unblinking, that gaze had stimulated Cabassac all the more. Hadn't Julieta always kept some small part of herself in reserve, Cabassac reflected, in a space to which he had no access whatsoever? He'd often thought that this reserve, this space, was what had drawn him so irresistibly to Julieta from the beginning. In the very first week they'd met, he'd jotted down in a leather-bound ledger book: 'Maybe it's not a person we fall in love with so much as a distance, a depth which that particular person happens to embody. Perhaps it's some inconsolable quality in that person, some unappeasable dimension that attracts one all the more forcibly.' Now, two years after Julieta's death, Cabassac found himself drawn even more irresistibly into those regions to which he had – indeed – no access whatsoever. No, none, that is, except in his dreams.

It wasn't until February of that second year that Cabassac came to the inevitable conclusion: on the very nights he ate truffles, he was given to dream of

Julieta, and abundantly so. February, what's more, happens to be the most delectable month for that capricious fruit. It also happens to be the time in which many truffles perish, victims of the long winter frosts. Only the most deeply rooted, most firmly embedded, manage to survive. Rare at the best of times, truffles become even rarer in February as the temperatures fall and the long, uninterrupted blasts of the winter mistral glaze the air with a lacquer so blue it's virtually black. On such days, the air itself seems frozen and the earth, impregnable.

Cabassac, nonetheless, felt enthralled. Having come to associate his sparse harvests with his prolific dreams, he knew he had unlocked the door to those most hidden regions. He'd done so, however, at the worst of moments. With the temperatures falling, the truffles had nearly vanished from their habitual haunts along the edge of the oak woods. Added to that, only a few weeks remained in the truffle season. The coldest moments of winter in Provence would often be followed by an especially precocious spring. He'd have to work rapidly now, Cabassac realized. He'd have to root out whatever tubers he could in the painfully little time that remained.

'One buried thing for another,' he often repeated to himself as he moved, each morning, over the frozen ground in his worn corduroys and battered lumber jacket. The truffle had come to spell image, apparition:

16

spell the surprisingly tall, austere figure of Julieta emerging out of so many vaporous particles, her gaze radiant and her black hair glossy in the sunlight. Sometimes, too, it spelled whispers, confessions, or simply the admission, on Julieta's part, of some long-suppressed yearning. Cabassac, of course, dreamt of his wife throughout the entire year, but only in brief glimpses, scattered frames, incoherent episodes. But under the influence of that winter tuber, his dreams – suddenly – expanded, deepened, grew far more poignant. For seemingly hours, the two of them in this dreamlife would bathe naked in waterfalls as they had once, or simply share the same work table together: two scholars locked in the mutual silence of a singular pursuit.

What's more, Cabassac soon discovered that his dreams were turning sequential: one episode would lead, infallibly, into the next. Just before falling asleep, he only needed to recall the very last minutes of his previous dream to be given – as if moments later – its running sequel. Recently, for instance, he'd dreamt of Julieta, her back turned, kneeling in a flower garden. It must have been summer, for her shoulders – broad but astonishingly svelte – were bare, tanned, and shimmering with perspiration. 'Philippe,' she called out, her face as if buried in flowers. Marigold, dahlia, foxglove virtually enveloped her like flowers in the enamel inlay of some miniature Renaissance locket.

'Philippe,' she called out once again, her shoulders still turned and the back of her head as if aureoled in all that enveloping florescence. Cabassac, in response, had knelt down, wrapped his arms about her waist, and pressed a cheek against the quick, shimmering puddle of her hair. 'What is it, my Julieta? *De que t'arribo?*' Even though he could hear her, feel her, even smell her sudden, resinous scent, she – in turn – clearly heard, felt, smelt perfectly nothing. She went on calling, nonetheless. And Cabassac, for his part, went on responding, reassuring, pressing himself against her shoulders, experiencing her physical presence every bit as much as if she were totally alive and he totally awake. Such a moment seemed to last indefinitely. Elastic in time, it expanded as if the two of them, the flower garden in which they found themselves, the very air, indeed, which surrounded that whole hallucinatory setting, existed in some warm, rich, viscous substance. Within that substance, their least gesture seemed buoyed, suspended. Seemed to exist in a sumptuous slow motion of its own.

'Philippe,' he'd hear repeatedly. By now, though, her voice would have begun fading. And Cabassac's hands, cupped over her hard adolescent breasts, would feel themselves slowly relinquish their hold. Together, the two of them began dissolving from that very matrix that had retained them throughout the dream's duration.

Within minutes, now, they vanished altogether: one into the netherworld that she inhabited; the other into the rooms, windows, landscapes of a life for which he'd lost all heart whatsoever.

February of that second winter Provence froze hard. The woods, white with ice, resembled more the woods in some high-contrast black-and-white negative. Nature itself seemed inverted. Only the splash of a tiny goldfinch, occasionally, brought some measure of color into that desolate landscape Cabassac – obsessively – worked through. By now, he'd have grown profoundly anxious. Having entered the very last weeks of the truffle season, desperate for yet another vision of Julieta (hadn't she called out his name, over and over, as if she had something – something essential – to tell him?), he went out, compulsively now, each and every morning. For three weeks running, though, he found nothing whatsoever: not a single, telltale fly. Not a sole deeply ensconced tuber. His dreams remained scattered, fragmentary, inconsequential. Not once had he entered that prolonged state of grace: that *dispousicioun*, as he himself liked to call it.

One afternoon, much to his own surprise, Cabassac found himself beating, thrashing at the wild grasses. Out of sheer frustration, he'd broken with ritual, with his own ceremonial sense of propriety, and begun

19

lashing out at one patch of frozen vegetation after another. 'Don't tell me you've vanished,' he muttered. 'Don't tell me you've gone back into all that shadow, got lost in all those endless veils of yours.' Cabassac, that very instant, was no longer addressing either the fly or the truffle but the very heart of his long-vanished beloved.

He'd have to wait, though, for the ground to thaw and the first timid signals of spring to break like so many flags from their hard little shell cases. He'd have to wait until the first wild almonds had begun blossoming, bringing with them a whole host of honeybees, before unearthing the last truffle. It lay between the pawlike roots of a holm oak at a depth of no less than forty centimeters. A richly faceted 'black diamond,' as they're occasionally called, this particular truffle had a wild, oily, provocative aroma. If a relationship could be established between the scent of a given tuber and the poignancy of the dream it was capable of provoking, then this very last truffle – Cabassac realized – was bound to be immensely effective. He had to wait, though. Held to a time-honored Provençal tradition, he had to remain patient for three full days while the truffle, sealed in a glass jar with three or six or even nine fresh eggs, infused those very eggs with its delectable aroma. Respecting the trinity in its own pastoral manner, this tradition was still scrupulously observed in most households throughout the region. Cabassac observed it himself knowing that thereby his dream would be all the greater.

And so, indeed, it was. Three nights later, he scrambled the sliced truffle together with three of those fully embalmed farm eggs and fried them to a strict minimum. In his tall, gloomy kitchen, seated at a table covered in oilcloth and lit by a low, overhanging wicker lampshade, he entered into his own private sacrament, eating his *brouiado de rabasso* in a state of total concentration. Mulling over each forkful, he refused to let a single note of that exquisite savor escape his palate. Biting lightly, then letting his tongue work its way into the aromatic mass, he marveled at that mysterious food, far more carnal, fleshy, gamelike than anything vegetal. The truffles, he recognized, were more the meat of some long-forgotten sacrifice than the fungus they were all too commonly considered.

Washing the ensemble down, now, with sips of a heavy, nearly granular red wine, Cabassac savored every bit as much the aftertaste as the taste itself. He let himself be drawn into the truffle's influence as into that of some gradual yet all-pervasive hypnosis. He ate lightly, that night. In fact, aside from the *brouiado* and two heavy slices of rye bread with which he swabbed his plate clean, he ate nothing more than a narrow wedge of moon-white goat cheese. Already, he began feeling his tensions ease, his nerves expand. Already, reassured by the savor of that earthen gland, he entered that languorous, deeply conducive state: that *dispousicioun*, as he called it.

Following a strict set of highly ritualized gestures, Cabassac then moved to a heavy straw-backed armchair, drank a deep bowl of verbena, leafed through a few pages of some philological report, and waited for the tall pendulum clock in his empty hallway to ring nine. At nine exactly, just as the pendulum – decorated with a garland of gold-plated roses – struck the hour, Cabassac retired. Upstairs, now, under the dark beamed ceiling of his bedroom, his bed alone testified to the attention he paid to the least preparatory detail. Not a pleat, not a single starched fold, neither of its puffed matching pillows, didn't lie like elements in some strict ceremonial arrangement. For ceremony, indeed, there was. No sooner had Cabassac slipped into his bed and turned off the light, feeling as he did the bulk of his body stretch to the very baseboard, than he began recapitulating each and every detail from his previous dream. Hadn't Julieta, in that dream, repeatedly called out his name? Hadn't he detected, by the very tone of her voice, a marked urgency? A need, as never before, to be heard? Recalling each and every instant, running them like a single, continuous band of electromagnetic tape through his memory, he quickly put himself to sleep. And, once asleep, found his previous dream fading rapidly into the next. Within minutes, Cabassac had resuscitated his Julieta. Drawn into his own oneiric litany, he found her once again kneeling in that very same garden, her shoulders glistening against a blaze of tall midsummer blossoms. This time, though, she turned, faced him. This time, she addressed him in a series of brief, cryptic phrases across that incommensurable distance.

'Philippe,' she called out. 'Come closer, Philippe.' Cabassac, that very instant, was running his hands through her shimmering, short-cropped hair. Julieta, however, had no way of knowing this.

'Closer,' she pleaded, as if Cabassac were standing on the opposite side of some profound abyss. 'Can you hear me, Philippe? Can you?'

More than merely hear her, Cabassac felt her, smelt her, indulged himself in the scent of those rich natural resins that issued from her every pore.

'Because there's something,' she went on, her voice still raised, projected into that distance, 'something that I have to tell you.'

'Tell me,' he whispered.

'Something wonderful, perfectly marvelous,' she called out, 'if only you'd come a bit closer.' Cabassac, by now, had come as close to Julieta as one living person can come to another. Conflated, indissociable, his body no longer his but part of that union that's ultimately neither's, no one's, he whispered into the warm mollusk of her ear, 'Tell me. Tell me, *ma Julieta.*'

She, however, went on calling and calling. Went on hoping that Cabassac would emerge out of that unsoundable distance, for she had 'something wonderful, perfectly marvelous,' that she wanted to tell him.

II

C abassac had first caught sight of Julieta during his introductory lecture on Provençal linguistics. In the dark gloomy auditorium where he offered up his luminous insights every year on that dying language, she'd taken a seat in the very back row. Cabassac, absorbed in making some preliminary remarks on the Gallo-Romanic origins of Provençal and oblivious for the most part of his auditors, had noticed her, none-theless, almost immediately. He might, in fact, have been drawn by the sheer radiance – the hive-like in-tensity – of her concentration. Taking note after note, she'd glance up, occasionally, less with her eyes, it seemed, than with her tall mineral forehead. Intense, totally absorbed in the subject itself, she circumscribed a space utterly her own.

For the duration of the lecture, Cabassac tried to keep his thoughts from lingering on that dark-haired stranger, seated in the farthest reaches of that somber lecture hall. But his gaze kept returning, nonetheless, to that same magnetic point, the point itself as if sparkling in a tight cluster of black facets. With each glance, furthermore, Cabassac drew a certain satisfaction. This highly attentive student was not merely listening but recording his each and every remark. His words, he realized, were entering the inner world of her thoughts, there where reflection, sensibility, lay secreted. Something of his, no matter how slight, had begun rooting, ruminating in those dark chambers within.

Week after week, lecture after lecture, he'd observe this same, solitary young woman take her seat in the last row of the auditorium, open her notebook, and begin jotting down page after page of lecture notes. Somewhere in midterm, he'd even remarked that she was left-handed: an observation that Cabassac treated as a somewhat small but cherished acquisition. Otherwise he knew nothing whatsoever about this attentive, highly applied, but perfectly remote student of his. It wasn't, in fact, until the very last lecture before the Christmas break that they actually met. The lecture itself, dealing with Provençal geo-phonetics – with the variations, that is, that exist between one dialectical area and another – had left a number of students curious about certain aspects of that puzzling, often contradictory subject. Immediately after the lecture, Cabassac found himself surrounded. Much to his surprise, she, too, had come to join the little circle. Biding her time, standing to one side, asking nothing for the moment, she waited for the others to conclude. It took, indeed, nearly half an hour for that little circle of young scholars to dissipate and for the two of them, finally, to find themselves face to face. Even then, though, she couldn't speak. Even then, she stood mute, staring at Cabassac not with her eyes but with that tall, luminous, mineral forehead of hers.

It was Cabassac, finally, who broke the silence, initiated the exchange. 'I've noticed you,' he found himself saying. 'You're always seated, aren't you, in the very last row of the auditorium?'

Her lips spread to form a slight, nearly imperceptible sign of acknowledgment. At the same moment, her gaze – matte, unfathomable – floated up from under that tall forehead to meet his.

'You seem to be taking a great many notes,' Cabassac continued, attempting to provoke a conversation by whatever means he could. 'I doubt that there's any student in this entire auditorium who takes notes as assiduously as yourself,' he added, filling the silence with whatever words that came to mind.

Once again, her lips spread. But this time, Cabassac noted, they spread a bit wider than before. They glistened as they did.

'What's more,' Cabassac went on, ready to commit

any number of improprieties, now, for the sake of filling that awkward silence, 'you're left-handed, aren't you? Yes, I've noticed that. I've watched you,' he confessed, 'writing page after page with that left hand of yours.'

Her lips spread even further, curling as they did at the very corners, but her gaze remained distant, remote, circumspect, filled with an irreducible resolve. As for Cabassac, he'd run out of words, out of small talk. Against every innate fiber in his being, he had no alternative, now, but to excuse himself. Excuse himself and be gone. He told this tall, perplexing stranger that he was running late. That he had an appointment, that afternoon, in Aix. That he was glad, though, that they'd met. That he made her acquaintance. That perhaps some other time they'd have yet another opportunity, as he put it, 'to exchange a few words.' Then, as he turned to leave, he added, almost as an afterthought, his coat already thrown over his shoulders: 'I have my car parked by the ramparts. Do you need a lift anywhere?'

Her response was barely perceptible. It came in the form of a nod, an affirmation so slight, so tenuous, so totally improbable that Cabassac couldn't believe that something potentially that meaningful could be expressed by something so manifestly insignificant. Yet there it was. And it was followed, just an instant later, by a tiny fluttering movement of her long, narrow hand, suggesting that Cabassac wait a moment while she fetched her things.

For Cabassac, that nod, that minuscule inclination of her forehead, came to mark – in retrospect – the very beginning of the rest of his life. Even then, in that exact moment, he dimly sensed the immense implications inherent in that smallest of gestures.

When she returned a full ten minutes later, she was carrying not only a student's book satchel but a plaid-covered suitcase. Without an instant's hesitation, Cabassac took the suitcase from the young woman's hand, and – with only the briefest of glances – led her through the dark university doorways and out onto the street. From there, the two of them walked briskly – their steps nearly matching, hers only a millisecond behind his – to Cabassac's car parked by the ramparts. They walked as if they'd taken that very walk together every day of their lives. As if nothing in the world could have been more natural. Even the silence they maintained as they walked – their every step nearly matching – seemed something complicitous. It was as if everything that might happen, now, had been decided, predetermined, from the very start.

Words came. Came gradually. With great deliberation, she began telling Cabassac bits and pieces about her life as they drove southward, now, towards Aix. He learned, for instance, that she'd been adrift for the past

31

two or three years, sleeping a bit everywhere: on a friend's sofa in one place, on a lover's bed in another. She'd even squatted all summer in a deserted university dormitory. More than by what she said, though, Cabassac was fascinated by how she said it. For she gave to each word a kind of weight, preponderance, as if the word not only expressed what it had to say, but – like some sonorous receptacle – contained what it said in its own magical vessel.

And so, choosing one word over another, hesitating here, precipitating there, editing her own speech a bit everywhere, she offered Cabassac a portrait of herself – of her own wayward existence – in which the words, seemingly, had far more consistency than the events themselves. Cabassac wasn't surprised to learn that she was an orphan and had been brought up by sisters in one rural convent after another. 'Prayers,' she murmured just then, recalling those very years, 'those long, unending prayers.' When Cabassac asked this perfect stranger sitting alongside him – her black hair flashing in the intermittent rays of midwinter sunlight that broke through the windshield – what she prayed for in those early years, she answered flatly, succinctly: 'That they'd end. That the prayers would end, once and for all.' Then, hesitating, searching for the word, the exact words to give shape to what, apparently, had been a shapeless existence, she added:

'That the prayers would end. End so that everything else could begin.' Out of a world of scrubbed floors and starched uniforms, out of the immense shadows cast by the nuns' immaculate headdresses, she'd waited for that long arduous period to come, at last, to a close.

'And did it?' Cabassac asked. 'Did it end?'

'No,' she said with a curt shake of her head. 'No, it never really did,' she added somewhat remorsefully. 'I'm still hoping, I suppose, that it might.'

Adrift, Cabassac thought to himself, moving from one apartment to the next, one lover to another, or simply gazing into her own disconsolate reflection in an endless sequence of identical reflections, hadn't she drifted into his lectures, as well, and now into this encounter, this exchange, this very moment in which the two of them funneled down the long corridor of a country road, syncopated by the presence, on either side, of so many stout, leafless plane trees? No, more than drifted, Cabassac corrected himself. He'd watched, all fall, how attentive she'd been to his lectures; how assiduously she'd taken notes. Something had drawn her, at first, into that auditorium; drawn her, that very afternoon, into his car, onto that road, and toward wherever the two of them might have been headed. Whatever it was, he concluded, it wasn't fortuitous.

In Aix, Cabassac took several philological studies out

of the well-stocked university library, met briefly with a colleague, and ran a few errands along the broad, stately Cours Mirabeau. During that time, this newfound companion, whose first name he still didn't know, whose age he could only guess as being, perhaps, twenty-five or twenty-six, followed him at no more than an instant's remove. She turned as he turned, sat as he sat, but always, he remarked, at a moment's – a millisecond's – interval. Hadn't he noticed that nearly imperceptible trait as they'd walked to his car along the ramparts hours earlier? That tiny interval, indeed, in-trigued him, for it expressed – in the midst of whatever had drawn her to Cabassac – a certain hesitation; a reserve, no matter how minute, in regard to whatever lay before them. Turning as he turned, sitting as he sat, she preserved, nonetheless, a distinct autonomy.

Silent for the most part, absorbing the sounds, the general atmosphere, the light falling across the rich ocherous façades of the *hôtels particuliers*, she was especially drawn by whatever she could convert, ar-ticulate in so many halting little phrases. 'Mandarins,' she declared – almost childishly – before an open fruit stand.

'Would you like some? Should we buy ourselves a bagful?' Cabassac proposed.

'Mandarins,' she repeated, a smile coming to her face. Quite clearly, she delighted more in the sound of that winter fruit than in the prospect of the fruit itself. Then, almost as an afterthought, she added: 'No, no thank you. It's such a pleasure, though, seeing them. Just seeing the little green flags of their leaves fluttering in the wind,' she said, pleased that she'd found a befitting metaphor for these very first fruits of the year.

The rest, Cabassac realized, would be simple, straight-forward. Wouldn't require any explanations whatso-ever. Driving back along the raised plains beyond Aix, the ground as if ruled by the rigorous black lines of the vine rows, he merely needed to describe his house – his great, ramshackle farmhouse – to this complicitous stranger. How he'd lived within its walls from the very day of his birth, a farm which had belonged to his parents and their parents and theirs again for at least eight generations; a household which had seen – along with all its births, baptisms, marriages, and deaths – the unremitting production of a full range of basic, indis-pensable human provisions. It was a farmhouse bulging with the memory of plucked fruit, threshed grain, smoked meats. A place that had not only fed itself and existed in a state of near total autarky, but had provided basic sustenance for countless others, as well. Sitting in the midst of its own granges, stables, chicken coops, it had fallen, however, into disrepair over the past half-century due to the steady migration – the rural exodus – of its inhabitants. No one was left to work its fields or, for that matter, inhabit the fifteen rooms of the farmhouse itself. No one, Cabassac explained, but an aged aunt, an 'agrarian relic,' as he described her.

'And pigeons?' the young woman asked. 'Doesn't someone there still keep pigeons?' In asking the question, she'd slipped into Provençal. Instead of employing the French *pigeons*, she'd used that far more indigenous term *pijouns*.

For Cabassac, this ever so slight divergence in the pronunciation of a single word meant a good deal more than a simple linguistic nuance. It spelled affinity. Declared kinship. 'No,' he replied, 'the pigeons have long since vanished,' he explained, slipping into Provençal himself. Indeed, from that moment on, he never addressed her in any other language but the language of that dying culture, its all but preempted sonorities. 'The pigeons vanished along with the wheat,' he explained. 'With all those endless wheat fields they once fed on. Gone, they're all gone, now.'

'*Pijouns*,' she murmured, pleasuring once again in the sound of a particular word, falling under the charm of its distinct resonance.

'As a boy,' Cabassac recalled, 'the pigeons greeted us every time we arrived at the farm with a great white cloud of wingbeats. The wingbeats sounded just like laundry. Like wind hitting a line of freshly hung, still dripping laundry.' At that very moment, though, as Cabassac's great, sprawling stone farmhouse came into sight, nothing greeted them but a tiny curlicue – a corkscrew – of blue smoke rising up out of a narrow chimneypot. Aside from that meager signal, the farmhouse itself appeared frozen in time. Even the long drive, lined on either side by stocky trunks of wintering mulberry, seemed little more than the memory of a once flourishing rural economy. Nothing in that spacious complex indicated the least passage of time except by its very dereliction.

Once inside, he led her to the kitchen, warm with its cast-iron stove on one side, its fireplace on the other. 'Wait here,' he said, 'while I make things ready.'

She gazed back, tall, guileless, the strap of her book satchel still twisted about her wrist. Once again, he noted how that gaze of hers seemed to emerge from under the ledge of her high, luminous forehead. '*Madamisello?*' he asked, for he still didn't know her first name.

'Julieta,' she murmured, a smile spreading across her lips.

'Here,' he said, 'you'll be more comfortable here, Julieta,' he exclaimed as he drew a heavy Provençal armchair up to the fireplace. He treated her, from the very start, with unfailing deference. Offered her, from that very first afternoon, the kind of attention one would give a visiting dignitary. Leading her to the armchair, now, while relieving her of her book satchel, Cabassac felt – that very moment – stirred by a dim recollection. In his early childhood, hadn't he led yet another tall, stately, yet estranged figure to that very same armchair? Immensely fragile, entering perhaps the very last weeks of her life, incapable at that stage of looking after another, least of all her own son, hadn't she radiated, just then, an indelible memory? No matter how faint, an ineffaceable recollection? What's more, didn't she have, as well, a shock of glistening black hair, a long Roman nose, a face that – heart-shaped – tapered into a perfectly delicate cleft chin? Well, didn't she, Cabassac kept asking himself as he excused himself, just then, and walked out.

In the next half hour, he managed to sweep and clean a vacant bedroom upstairs, open its shutters and empty out its shelves, make its broad blue wrought-iron bed with the very best linen he possessed, and deck its bare bathroom racks with fresh towels. Lastly, he hauled a pair of matching commodes into the bedroom and placed – on top of each – not only a lace doily but, at the very center, a cut crystal vase. It being December, there were no flowers, of course. Still he placed the vases on top of the doilies and the doilies on top of their commodes in way of 'provision,' as he called it. 'For all the flowers to come.'

Thus, Julieta was received. Thus, that late-December afternoon, she was installed. Along with a bed, a bedroom, and all the accompanying conveniences, she was given every conceivable attention that one person can bestow on another. Cabassac's infatuation, compounded by years of unmitigated solitude, had come to focus on this student with an intensity – a devotion – that astonished even Cabassac himself. There was nothing that this confirmed bachelor, this *vieux garçon*, wouldn't do for her, either. Beginning on that very afternoon, he cooked for her, served her his simple yet delectable country dishes, brought heated towels to her bathroom door, and read to her: read page after page of poetry in that nearly extinct language that both of them cherished as they lingered about an open oakwood fire. Cabassac had prepared the fire, as well, hauled in its wood, and set twig, branch, and log ablaze, while his adored Julieta sat, solidly ensconced in a high, tufted armchair, her long legs tucked under her like a nesting flamingo's.

'*Encara un pauc d'aigardent?*' he asked her. 'Another drop of spirits?' They'd been sipping quince liqueur from tiny shot glasses as Cabassac read and Julieta – thoroughly absorbed – listened.

With a brief shake of her head that set her black hair shimmering, she said no, that she'd had enough. Then, with only the slightest of smiles, she added: 'But why?'

'Why what?' Cabassac responded, somewhat puzzled.

'Why everything? Why this liqueur? This fire? These poems?' After a moment's hesitation, she went on, expressing herself as she often would in a series of clipped, breath-bitten phrases: 'It's so much. So very much. These rooms, this house, the very bed I sleep in. But why? What are you doing it for?' she asked, gazing across at Cabassac, his steel-framed glasses reflecting the light from the open fire.

But there was no way Cabassac could answer her. For that matter, there was no way he could answer even himself. Somewhere, though, lingering along the very edge of his earliest, infantile memory, lay that other figure: that frail, stately, ineffaceable presence. Like a cameo, he thought, carved into consciousness itself. Like a medallion, deeply embedded. It was all that remained of his mother, her hand, occasionally, grazing his cheek or pressing, suddenly, against his three-year-old shoulder for some kind of support for her own rapidly failing condition. An image, he thought, a single, tenuous image. But isn't it this, finally, that kindles desire: an all but vanished memory? This, finally, that another, a perfect stranger, sets ablaze with nothing more nor less than a certain coincidental resemblance? This that, quite unwittingly, Julieta had released? She, who was half his age, who could easily

40

have been his daughter, had been elevated, on coincidence alone, to the rank of beloved.

'I don't know. I can't say exactly,' Cabassac finally answered. 'But sometimes, seeing you seated – like this evening, for instance – your legs tucked under and your hands running through your hair, you seem to mean more to me,' he confessed, 'than anything on earth.' In saying this, the tone of his voice was as flat, factual, as it was boundlessly reverential.

Unfazed, Julieta gazed back.

'More, certainly, than anything I can express,' he said as he rose, now, to his feet.

Thoroughly undaunted, she continued to gaze back, offering Cabassac all the unfathomable wealth of a single, singular, inscrutable smile.

'Far more . . .' he reiterated as he walked over to her armchair and kissed the very top of her shiny black hair. 'Good night,' he whispered, lingering in that position for an instant more than he might. '*Bono nive*' as he put it, using as always that dying idiom in which the two of them ineluctably edged toward an intimacy of their own.

It was at this time – in the very first days of their relationship – that Cabassac wrote in the tall, leather-bound ledger that he kept: 'Maybe it's not a person we fall in love with so much as a distance, a depth which

that particular person happens to embody.' For Cabassac, distance – depth – was constituted, he'd come
to realize, by the all but vanished image of that
founding presence, that beloved figure: she who'd
established, in turn, the criteria for every other presence. Every other figure. Had anyone ever answered
to that hallucinatory description as perfectly as Julieta?
he asked himself. Anyone's portrait fit, so ideally, that
empty frame? There'd been others, of course. Cabassac
had even had a long-standing liaison with an immensely kind, cultivated *bourgeoise* from Bormes-les-Mi-
mosas. She'd not only made herself available, but
catered to his every need, lavished – night and day –
an unending amount of attention on Cabassac's slightest whim, appetite, inclination. For seven consecutive
years, she was, in the fullest sense of the word, devoted
to this brooding, pensive, heavyset scholar. The liaison,
however, had dissolved on its own. Had failed, Cabassac could only feel, out of an absence of that depth,
dimension, that had drawn him, so resolutely, towards
Julieta. For Julieta, if anything, haunted those very
reaches. Wandered about in those very wastelands in
which nothing if not language served to mark space,
indicate direction. Within those immensities, she'd
select a nominal here, a participle there, as others
might pluck marigolds or medicinal herbs or the
speckled heads of mushrooms. Otherwise, she seemed

to idle in an expanse altogether exempt: an expanse, however, that not only fascinated Cabassac with its emptiness but stimulated – excited – him as well. For there, in those shifting landscapes, he was every bit as knowledgeable as she herself was bereft, in need. From the very first, he wanted to fill her with sound, sprinkle her long silences with a plethora of spoken particles. Wanted to occupy those amorphous immensities with every articulated cell of his being. Julieta, in turn, was only too ready to receive, accept, assimilate. That very week, for instance, Cabassac gave her a little tutorial touching upon certain dialectical permutations to be found in the Alpes-de-Haute-Provence: the euphonious 'a,' for example, in words such as *aperamount*, signifying as it does, in those regions, 'high up,' 'up there,' 'by the heights.' He watched her as she reiterated that very word in perfect silence, spreading her lips about the initial syllable, puffing them about the second, then rounding them about the third as if she were blowing a kiss into sheer air. '*Aperamount*,' she uttered out loud, now, fascinated by that very adverb, treating it more as some kind of key that might, potentially, allow entry into some otherwise inaccessible area of her obliterated past.

'*Meno me aperamount*,' she then said in a sudden burst of impetuosity. 'Take me upland,' she repeated. It wasn't a request so much as a declaration: a caprice that had taken on the unexpected form of a command. 'Yes, *aperamount*, that's where I want to go . . .'

So promise her he did, for there was virtually nothing Cabassac wouldn't do for this adored yet remote, perfectly estranged houseguest of his. 'As soon as my teaching schedule permits, I promise you, we'll take to the high plateaux. Yes, we'll drive upland together, *aperamount*.'

Julieta was scarcely listening. She was running the sound of that very word over her lips, then tracing her lips with the tip of a long, elongated finger as if to make sure that the sound really existed. That it had a physiognomy entirely its own.

The word, quite clearly, had struck a chord, for that very evening Julieta came and joined Cabassac on a deep-set sofa where he'd been reading a dense philological study on irregular verbs in the Rhône delta. She arrived silently, wearing woolen socks and a long woolen bathrobe, and sat herself not only alongside but against Cabassac more as a cat might, seeking some form of creature comfort for itself, than as a woman in search of affection. Cabassac, instinctively, understood this. Julieta, a full twenty-five years younger than he, could easily have been his child. Furthermore, she was his student, and Cabassac would never have violated the traditional teacher–student relationship which he himself had always respected in an austere if somewhat unquestioning manner. His love had taken on the form of a chaste veneration from the very first. Motivated, no doubt, by a deep-seated taboo, he'd come to idolize this tall, black-haired stranger who moved about his house, shared his meals, observed the very same schedule as he did every bit as much as if she'd been his wife or, at least, his mistress.

Running her shoulder up against his chest, now, and her head against his cheek, she stretched her arms out – catlike, once again – and murmured '*aperamount*' in a single, lighthearted exhalation.

'Yes,' Cabassac assured her, 'just as soon as I've finished preparing my next few lectures, I promise you that the two of us will travel upland. Take long, extensive field trips onto the raised plateaux.'

'Because,' she said as if she were thinking out loud, 'there's something, something there, I'm fully convinced.'

'Like what?' he asked her.

'Something that's always drawn me. Pulled me towards it,' she told him. 'Summers, for instance, when I came free of all those convents, I'd hitchhike up to Barcelonnette, find myself some summer job, do anything – pitch hay, milk goats, make goat cheese in those churning wheels – just to stay at those altitudes. Stay as long as the summer lasted.' She pulled free of Cabassac, just then, and went to stand by the open fire, leaning a long hip against the adjoining wall.

'Words, too,' she went on. 'How I loved listening to the words, the old words. It's as if that whole landscape happened twice: once before one's eyes, and once again in the language of its peasants, shepherds. Yes, the mountains, the high pastures, the waterfalls that fell, all summer, through their own shimmering veils. They'd turned into words. Wonderful receptacles.' It was, of course, words that had drawn Julieta to Cabassac from the very first. That had drawn her through the doors of the university to Cabassac's parked car, only days earlier. That had led her, finally, to this ramshackle farmhouse with its single, corkscrew twist of blue smoke rising out of one of its innumerable chimneypots. For Cabassac, there'd never been any doubt, either. Julieta's interest in Provençal linguistics, he was fully aware, was something far more than academic. It had something to do with those altitudes. Those spaces. Had they, he wondered, stirred something earlier than memory in this young woman? This orphan? Had they triggered, at some unconscious level, the reminiscence of some long-lost childhood? Some otherwise obliterated heritage?

She went on to tell him about an adventure – a *calignage* – that she'd had that past summer. 'There'd been others, of course, with boys, men, all summer.

46

Once, even, with an elderly *ferraiaire*, a dealer in scrap metal, who gave me a guided tour through his scrap heaps – a lecture, really, and in Provençal what's more – of that whole derelict world of his. Yes, scythes, sickles, plowshares, rusting away in one heap after another. He taught me everything I needed to know about those lost trades, abandoned professions. Oh, you learn things in the mountains, you truly do,' she exclaimed, poking the fire, now, and bringing its embers to squirt, bright gold. 'But it's not him, not the *ferraiaire* I wanted to tell you about. Not the three, four nights I spent in his little hovel until my whole body began smelling of rust, of rotting metal, no, not him, but the leaf-pickers. But the morning I hiked along the high plateau over Valensole and spotted them, half a kilometer off, picking mulberry leaves for their silkworms. There must have been at least seven of them, that morning – seven women – chattering away as they picked, stuffing those fat, heart-shaped leaves into big, billowing pillow-cases. It's a woman's world, of course, a woman's economy, picking those leaves and especially then, in the very last weeks of rearing silkworms, when those little monsters turn voracious. That particular morning, those seven women became eight. They took me in. In exchange for stuffing their pillowcases with mulberry leaves, they fed me, lodged me – well out of sight, I gather, from their husbands. One of them, in fact, wanted me for herself.

It didn't matter either. It didn't matter in the least. It was like having a wild passionate mother of one's own, a frenzied parent who'd bring me – once she'd satisfied herself, straightening her skirt and pulling straw from her hair – tall glasses of goat's milk and bowl after bowl of fresh raspberries. I loved it, in fact. I loved all that unending attention,' she confessed, 'and kept wishing that it would never end, that adventure. But why,' she asked, suddenly circumspect, 'why am I telling you all this?'

'Go on,' Cabassac urged her.

'I never thought I'd tell anyone.'

'Go on, go on,' he said in a near whisper. 'Tell me.'

'I never thought – I guess – that I'd ever meet anyone I could tell,' she murmured as she walked towards him, now, and Cabassac, in response, rose to receive her, to hold her in his arms as a kind of substitute parent himself. And, as he did, as he brought her long body taut against his, he once again thrilled to that rich resinous scent that her entire body exuded. He recognized, just then, in that natural effulgence, not a maritime resin, not even one reminiscent of the Bas Provence that they inhabited, but one redolent of the massive fir, spruce, and silver pine of those elevated plateaux that kept drawing Julieta so ineluctably upwards. *Aperamount*, he murmured to himself. *Aperamount*, he kept murmuring and murmuring as he held

Julieta stock still against him and exulted in that rich sylvan scent that she emitted.

One morning, Philippe Cabassac heard Julieta laughing. She was downstairs, helping his aunt prepare one of the Thirteen Desserts for the traditional Provençal Christmas dinner, when he overheard the two of them laughing light-heartedly. This aunt, who lived in a wing of her own in that wide, ramshackle farmhouse, had been widowed from an early age, and left with an only child, a daughter named Magalie. But Magalie had moved to Canada several years earlier in search of a job, leaving her mother to live totally alone. Cabassac, alone himself (his parents had passed away several years earlier, and he'd recently broken off his seven-year-long liaison with that all-too-devoted companion), had welcomed this nearly deaf, dotty aunt of his into his huge, drafty farmhouse. He'd done so, indeed, as much for his own sake as hers. For he, too, needed companionship. From the very first day, however, Cabassac had discovered that his aunt, Tanto Mirèio, needed nothing whatsoever. With her own irascible habits and her mind half astray, she was perfectly happy wandering about her part of the house dressed head to foot in black with nothing but a few purple polka dots sprinkling her head scarf as a concession of sorts to an otherwise long-vanished femininity. Refusing every form of modern

49

convenience, she drew her own water from the well, cooked her own meals over an open fire, and kept an impeccable vegetable garden that looked – from a certain distance – like a Byzantine mosaic.

With Julieta's arrival, however, she'd come scuffling more and more often into Cabassac's part of the house. She'd bring whole baskets of winter vegetables from her garden, most especially – at that time of year – long lime-green branches of chard. Growing tall as a scarecrow at the edge of every Provençal garden, this edible thistle with its succulent stalks and fanglike leaves marked the end of the season, the year, the solar cycle.

'Magalie,' his aunt called out, 'look at Magalie,' she said, pointing to Julieta. 'Just look, isn't she lovely, my Magalie!'

And look he did. Never had he seen Julieta as beautiful as then, standing in the middle of the kitchen floor, her arms filled with a great bouquet of that white thistle, and her head thrown back in laughter. 'Just look,' his aunt went on as if she were pointing towards her very own masterpiece.

As for Julieta, she quite clearly adored playing Magalie. Cast, even miscast, as someone's daughter, *anyone's* daughter, she delighted in the role she'd been assigned by that dear, half-delirious, ersatz mother of hers. With Julieta's head thrown back in laughter and her long, swanlike neck dappled in winter sunlight, Cabassac could only look on in amazement.

'Just look. For me, you're not a day older than on the morning of your first communion. Remember when I rubbed you down in spirits of honeysuckle and dressed you up like a little princess in starched crinoline? You kept stuffing things into that very first brassière of yours: a kitchen sponge, toilet paper, anything that might have given you just a bit of contour. Oh Magalie, remember?'

Julieta beamed back at Tanto Mirèio. 'Of course I do,' she said, unabashed. 'How could I have forgotten?' And it struck Cabassac, that very instant, that Magalie and Julieta might indeed have shared many of the same adolescent experiences even if one had grown up in a home and the other in a series of convents.

'You began bleeding, too, that very same week . . .'

'I felt so proud, so very proud.'

'You bled more than most girls, I remember. You bled and bled . . .'

'I tried tasting it, too. I thought it would taste of something mysterious. Even magical,' she said. 'And it did. It really did.'

'You kept bleeding, I remember, and I kept scrubbing. Your bedsheets, your nightshirts. Oh Magalie, it was just like yesterday. Not a single day more.'

The two of them gazed at one another totally

enthralled. They'd entered, by now, into a deep fictive complicity together. No matter how illusory their relationship, each managed to play the part of the other's missing personage. The bereaved mother, the abandoned daughter, chattered away in the kitchen, shelled almonds together by an open fire or prepared long white slices of that edible thistle for the upcoming Christmas feast.

'Just look,' Tanto Mirèio went on, proud of this daughter's – this lovely, lost daughter's – resuscitation. Then, in all her excitement, she brought a plastic wreath out of the cellar – the kind Provençal traditionally lay at the foot of a tombstone – and, pulling it apart, pinned a plastic rose in Julieta's hair, then another through a buttonhole in her heavy woolen cardigan. At this time of year, indeed, there were no other flowers available than those stored in the dark vaulted larders below.

'Here, too,' Tanto Mirèio exulted as she decked Julieta now with one plastic flower after another, not only in every buttonhole in her heavy woolen cardigan but about her belt, the pockets of her blouse, behind each of her naked ears. And yes, once again, in her hair a splash of pink in the midst of all that shimmering black.

'My Magalie, my lovely Magalie! Just look at my lovely girl who's returned home at last!' the old woman exulted, clasping her hands together and sighing in satisfaction.

Cabassac gazed on in amazement. Julieta, standing still as a statue in the midst of the kitchen floor, barbed in all that funereal blossom – those rigid, unwilting, odorless roses – had never appeared so radiant. So profoundly alive.

Mornings, occasionally, he'd hear her bathing. With the water pipes in her own bathroom frozen, she'd come barefoot down the narrow corridor – its red, lozenge-shaped floor tiles long gone unwaxed – and draw water from the only functioning bathtub in that rambling, broken-down farmhouse. The bathroom itself adjoined Cabassac's bedroom. And, as he lay in bed, he couldn't help but imagine Julieta undressing, then slipping into that enamel tub that stood on four immutable cast-iron lion's paws. Slapping water over each shoulder or drawing her legs out – one at a time – to lather them in a slick glistening film of suds created sounds that Cabassac, in the next room, could only visualize, translating each of their distinctive noises into evocative pictures. Those pictures left him feeling both disturbed and aroused. This was particularly true when Julieta finally emerged from the bath in a single, eruptive cataract of soapy water. At those very moments, Cabassac could only imagine her as some tall, Junoesque figure, standing marbled – head to foot – in that streaming water except at the very base of her long, boylike torso where the water caught in a narrow shrub, a vortex of bunched wires that caused Cabassac to hesitate before qualifying that area as pubic. Puritanical as he was impassioned, protective as he was enamored, he found that he'd entered into total contradiction with himself. Every week, he felt more and more drawn, captivated by this svelte, elusive houseguest of his whom he'd brought under his roof, taken into his custody not as some potential mistress but as a damaged soul gone astray and in desperate – if undeclared – need of shelter.

He lay there, morning after morning, listening to the scarcely perceptible sounds of Julieta dressing. A zipper here, the distinctive rub of corduroy there, the crinkle of a heavily starched blouse yet there again. He listened to each of these discrete sounds as a librettist might, his attention fixed, fixated, absolute. He'd hear the squeak of Julieta's fingertips as they rubbed vapor off the surface of the bathroom mirror, and could only ima-gine, as he did, her tall, heart-shaped face emerging – flushed from the warm bath – into the midst of that radiant oval. She who wore no make-up would be applying – he could only imagine – some facial cream over her raised cheekbones or across that tall, mineral forehead of hers.

Moments later, she'd have left the bathroom and taken the narrow corridor back to her bedroom. As soon as she had, Cabassac would rise, dress as quickly as he could, and enter the hot, still steamy bathroom himself. But it wasn't the heat, the steam, or the warm bath that Cabassac had come for but that radiant oval: to see those broad, hastily drawn half-circles that Julieta had traced, only moments earlier, across the steamy surface of the mirror. No sooner had Cabassac removed his glasses and brought his heavyset head level with that oval than he peered, not into his own reflection, but into what he could only imagine as the fast-fading residue of hers: not into the violet of his own imploring gaze but the granular brown of her erratic, repeated, self-searching glances. '*Bèn-ama*,' he murmured, now, as he brought his lips flush against that rapidly dissolving vision. '*Bèn-ama, bèn-ama*,' he repeated until the hallucinatory presence of his adored orphan, his estranged idol, had vanished altogether. Until nothing was left in that radiant oval but Cabassac himself, murmuring to no one, now, his lips flush against perfectly nothing except their own empty, relentless entreaties.

By mid-January, classes resumed. The two of them would drive into Avignon together but separate at the city ramparts out of simple propriety. That way, they'd enter the lecture hall a few minutes apart. No one, though, detected anything suspect, irregular: any trace of the curious, asymmetric complicity they'd entered into. Julieta and Cabassac were far too private, furthermore, to arouse suspicion. Self-enveloped, shrouded in silence, neither was likely to stir rumor. Cabassac had to remind himself, however, not to let his gaze get caught on Julieta's countenance; remind himself to keep his eyes moving across the auditorium as he delivered one luminous discourse after another, tracing, just then, the history of the Felibrige, that erudite circle of Provençal scholars, in their crepuscular, *fin de siècle* struggle to keep that dying culture alive.

Weekends, though, were something else. Having prepared his lectures for the rest of the school year, Cabassac was free, at last, to take Julieta upcountry. To travel *aperamount*: into those regions that drew her, that is, with such a magnetic attraction. Every weekend, the two of them would crowd into Cabassac's little Renault, and visit some remote area of Haute Provence. There, as ethnolinguists, they'd interview peasants, blacksmiths, country priests as to the local pronunciation of a given phoneme or a slight syntactical variation to be found in some time-worn, wind-worn, death-worn dictum still in circulation. Not unlike entomologists collecting scarabs, they went about every weekend, now, collecting sounds. For there, in those high, isolated Alpine communities, still lingered some of the earliest vestiges of that Gallo-Romanic language.

'Breath relics,' Cabassac called them. They'd been preserved at those very altitudes across ten centuries of human existence by nothing less than penury, drought, and hailstones: by what the peasants still called three months of hell (*tres meses d'infert*) and nine months of winter (*noou meses d'uveart*). Within such an arduous world, the words themselves had circulated like a precious currency, an evanescent gold. Used sparingly, they were often the only means of exchange these mountain people possessed. In so many breath-bitten segments, they had cultivated a language that spoke almost exclusively in terms of felling timber and sluicing water, honing sickles and stacking hay, fumigating beehives and preparing unguents, infusions, and herbal remedies. Cabassac himself had compiled an entire lexicon devoted to nothing but grain. It included every word he'd managed to collect in regard to the grain's harvesting, threshing, winnowing; in regard, finally, to how those quintessential kernels got milled into flour alongside some frothy, splashing mountain cascade.

'Hardly a single word, though,' he confided to Julieta one day, 'expresses sentiment. Given the harshness of their lives, there wasn't room for expressing what they felt.' The two of them were seated, just then, at a café table in a small perched village, high within the Provençal Alps.

'Sometimes, though, I'm afraid of those silences,' Julieta confessed. 'Of all the things they *didn't* say, *didn't* acknowledge. All the secrets they kept even from themselves.' Cabassac looked across the café table at Julieta, her gaze guileless and her hair shimmering black in its own natural lacquer. She sat as alert – vigilant – as some elegant water bird perched on a stray bit of driftwood.

. . . *all the secrets they kept even from themselves*: her words went on ringing through Cabassac's thoughts. Quite apart from the semantic issues involved in such lacunae, Cabassac couldn't help but think of the silences – the secrets – that surrounded Julieta herself: her birth, her immediate abandonment, her entire childhood passed in one rural orphanage after another. Hadn't she virtually been born into a world of omissions, swaddled in the very cloth of so many inaudible whispers?

'So that when I find a word,' she continued, 'it's like finding a tiny space . . . a room, a niche, an alcove even. That's what I love. What I love finding. A word in the midst of all that emptiness.'

'More *tisano?*' he asked. The two of them were drinking verbena tea, its leaves freshly gathered from a tiny terraced garden alongside. Julieta, in response, smiled affirmatively.

Now as he poured that jade-green tea not into a cup,

not even into a bowl, but into the traditional *mountag-nardo* receptacle, the water glass, he realized as never before the significance for Julieta of that lost language. Only there, in that abandoned grammar, in those obsolescent participles, would she ever come to recognize and, in recognizing, ground herself in a birthright, a birthplace, a legitimacy of her own. It wasn't a master's degree she was after, he recognized, but an identity. In response, he wanted to fill her with those very words; feed her – this great, elegant water bird – with an abundance of sonorous morsels. Weren't words, language, his only entry: his only means of penetrating all that elusiveness, breaking into that otherwise locked receptacle and depositing, as he did, the whirring seed of so much articulated syllable?

He gazed, now, at the way the bright Alpine light reflected blue off the black of Julieta's shimmering hair. As he did, he felt – quite suddenly – her fingers as if toying with his. Felt her turning his hands over by the very fingertips, first to one side, then the other.

'They're just like his,' she murmured more to herself than to Cabassac. 'But exactly,' she uttered in total amazement.

'Like whose?' he queried.

Julieta was too preoccupied examining Cabassac's hands – first on one side, then the other – to hear Cabassac's question, let alone answer it.

'Whose hands?' Cabassac insisted. 'Whose hands do mine remind you of?' he asked, provoked by Julieta's sudden fit of curiosity.

'My father's,' she said in something scarcely more than a whisper. 'My father's hands,' she murmured as she went on inspecting Cabassac's as a botanist might the veins of some perfectly unique tropical leaf formation. In fact, running her index finger, that very instant, over the lines of his outstretched palms, she could easily have been mistaken for a fortune-teller if it weren't her own fortune she was attempting to read.

'I've begun dreaming,' she whispered, gazing into his open palms as into a bowl. 'In dream after dream, night after night, I've begun seeing him: seeing my very own father for the first time in my life. Not his face, exactly. For his face always seems shrouded, as if veiled, in shadows. No, his face never comes entirely clear. His hands, though, his hands emerging out of the sleeves of some immaculately clean workshirt, those – at least – I can see. See clearly. Night after night, his hands appear and they're exactly like these,' she repeated, running her fingertips over his palms as over two freshly ex- cavated archeological curiosities. And, as she did, Ca- bassac couldn't help but clamp those very hands shut about hers, pressing them with a fervor – a desperation – that surprised even himself. Their gazes met in that same instant: his heated, enthralled; hers intrigued, inquisitive, gazing not exactly at Cabassac but directly through him as if she were waiting for something located immediately behind the screen of his forehead, deep-set eyes and solid chin to appear at long last. To materialize once and for all.

It was spring before it actually happened: before they actually occurred as a couple, partook in that phenomenon that's neither one's nor the other's but exists in the mutuality – the mystery – of that simultaneous relinquishment. It happened almost by accident. They'd been visiting one outlying area of Haute Provence after another, collecting sounds, adages, whole narratives as they went, interviewing some of the last practitioners of that nearly extinct mountain idiom. They did so as devoted scholars. Even if one of them happened to be an authority on that very subject and the other a relative novice, they both shared a common – even a passionate – interest in gathering whatever they could of those fading grammatical particles: what had once constituted, in fact, a common currency for an entire human society.

That morning, as they traveled upland, *aperamount*, Cabassac had a distinct sense that they were approaching – drawing nearer and nearer to – something that they each, in their own manner, most ardently sought. They'd gradually grown magnetized to those altitudes, pasturelands, sheepfolds: to the last surviving circum-scriptions of that vanishing culture. Now, as Cabassac drove, he'd steal glances from time to time of Julieta's handsome profile. With her cleft chin slightly raised and her long, latinate nose in pure silhouette, she looked more like some antique cameo, Cabassac thought to himself. Like the carving of some maenad – some mountain sprite – you'd only expect to find in effigy. No, Cabassac suddenly corrected himself, no she doesn't. She doesn't remind you of anyone, in fact, if not the one person you can scarcely remember. If not that frail, stately invalid no older than Julieta herself, dying of some obscure cancer only three years after having given birth to her only child. Yes, she whom you'd led to the armchair by the fireplace, and who'd left as impression – no matter how vague, ephemeral – the most ineffaceable memory of your life. What is it then? Cabassac asked himself. What are we acting out, Julieta and myself? What is this pale, flickering screen of vaguely resemblant figures in which we each seem to perceive our own parent? The father she found in reading my hands? The mother who reappears each time I catch a glimpse – no matter how fleetingly – of her handsome profile?

Through the half-open windows that sent Julieta's black hair streaming past her temples in a single unin-terrupted flow, Cabassac could smell – at the very same moment – the rich, alkaline scent of freshly plowed earth, just beyond. It was spring. And if spring arrived late at those altitudes, it came – as all long-awaited things – as an utter blessing. Cabassac felt this intensely. Climbing past the last farmlands, the curves of the road espousing – on one side – those of a frothy Alpine torrent a full fifty meters beneath, and – on the other – stand after stand of ruler-straight mountain ash, they went from the blinding white brilliance of the sun before them into tunnel after tunnel of seemingly impenetrable shadow. Lightness and dark, brilliance and obscurity, alternated on that high Alpine road like elements in some arcane metaphysical puzzle.

Now, in quitting one of those dark passages, Cabassac noted that Julieta had her eyes fixed, once again, on his hands. They lay curled, tightly clamped about the steering wheel. Passing into a new series of shadows, they'd appear and disappear as the car wended its way toward a mountain pass, flashing on and off like an illumination. With his eyes glancing at hers, and hers at his hands, he couldn't help but ask:

'Are you still having those dreams?'

'Always,' she answered in a rush of breath, her eyes fixed, now, on the road before her.

'About him?'

She nodded. 'About him,' she said in almost a whisper, 'but about here, too. About him in places like this where everything smells of sawdust. Of sawdust and woodsmoke. Of skeins, too, of freshly shorn wool. Yes, about him in places like this: his hands, his sleeves, his impeccable plaid workshirt as he chops wood or sips – in some smoky café – mountain alcohol out of a thimble-size shot glass. That's exactly what I dream about,' she told him in a single rush of irrepressible words.

For Cabassac, there could be no question. Julieta was dreaming of things that she could otherwise in no way have remembered: her natural father, the trades he practiced, the very smells of the land – the arduous landscape – into which she'd once been born. Weren't her features alone, Cabassac asked himself, distinctly Provençal? If, indeed, place can be said to determine physiognomy – to shape, that is, one's physical characteristics – couldn't Julieta's features be considered not merely Provençal but – more exactly – Alpine Provençal? Everything about her, Cabassac recognized, was redolent of altitude, raised plateaux. Even her inherent austerity, inscribed in that tall, luminous forehead, spoke of rocks and cascades, of wild, resinous stands of pinewood. Spoke, too, of whispers and long-guarded family secrets, of salted meats hanging from rafters and ceilings black with an unending winter's wood smoke; of men boisterous over the green beans they'd staked in some heated card game, and women –

yes, women – stashing away against the ever-impending famine tiny bits of tooth-bitten gold they'd acquired from the clandestine sale of what was once called 'lunar wheat.' Spoke, too, of the first, fat, long-awaited omelettes of spring, and sliced apples laid out on boards to dry in the sun. Of the sound of beekeepers, beating their cauldrons to draw their swarm – their runaway swarm – back into those low, latticed, tin-roofed beehives. Spoke, too, of feeding the hog charcoal the night before its slaughter for cleansing its intestines, of the bath in which its carcass was boiled the day after, and the murmurs – reverential – of a whole hamlet standing about, witnesses to that ceremony that hadn't entirely lost something of the sacramental. Of chaff, too. Of chaff flying like sparks in a high wind, the wheat being beaten, threshed, so that the grain itself would tumble to the ground and the weightless husks blow in the wind like burnished dust. All this was written into every fold, trait, contour of Julieta's physiognomy, her beautiful face but the extreme concentrate of all the many forces that high, arduous region had brought to bear.

That morning, they headed out as they often had in search of what Cabassac called 'breath relics.' The morning itself had begun normally, even perfunctorily enough. They left, as always, well before dawn and reached Sisteron – the river citadel – by sunrise. From there, they crossed the Durance and began gradually rising through field after field of ruled, immaculately pruned lavender. Gradually, too, they moved from a world of ocher-red roof tiles, characteristic of Mediterranean cultures, to one of overlapping layers of blue Alpine slate. Indeed, they could measure their very altitude as they went by the roofing alone, for soon after passing through the last, scattered hamlets gabled in that overlapping shingle, they came to yet another covering: slabs of heavy, moss-eaten stone. There, those ungainly, stratified sections appeared to overwhelm – virtually crush – the tiny, high-pitched mountain hovels they were called upon to protect.

There was nothing about that beautiful spring morning that was particularly different, particularly auspicious. As two dedicated scholars, they went about their business as usual, interviewing, recording their sources, drafting field notes wherever they went. That day, they were particularly intent on tracking down any last, lingering phonetic traces of a folk custom attached to the many water mills in that mountain region. For the water mills had traditionally been named onomatopoetically: after the particular sounds that their rotating wooden water paddles made as they ground wheat to flour between two massive, monolithic millstones. By simple mimesis, each of the water mills had acquired not only a name but often a rhyme, a verset exclusively its own.

So it was with the water mill near Larches along the Italian frontier, which they'd finally reached, that day, in driving through those deep, successive tunnels of Alpine shadow. The water mill itself hadn't functioned for over a century, but the lovely epithet by which it had once been known continued to circulate in the memory of the oldest people in the area. The very oldest of all, a certain Madame Chabaud – tiny, stooped, with eyes as blue as her faded blue apron – received the two of them on her narrow, sunlit balcony overlooking the mountains just beyond. Serving them *génépi*, a wormwood alcohol, in minuscule eyecup glasses, the glasses catching fire against the flat, penetrating rays of sunlight, Madame Chabaud declared that there was one epithet in particular – one that was especially poignant (*pèrtoucant* was the term she used), if only her memory would serve her in good stead. As they sipped their drinks, they watched the old lady sew, attempting – as she did – to recall that lost epithet. It was Julieta who first noticed that the old lady, in fact, wasn't sewing but unsewing. She was unthreading stitch by stitch the seam of some exhausted bit of clothing, recuperating as she went nothing more nor less than the precious thread itself.

'*Calou ou cales*,' she began murmuring, more to herself, at first, than to either Julieta or Cabassac. Smiling, now, she repeated the same refrain over and

67

over, reciting it like some kind of nursery rhyme: '*Calou ou cales, li voou, li vas*':

> I tumble down, you tumble down;
> I go under, you go under.

'That's it,' she told them. 'That's what the wooden paddles of the water mill at Bellon once said. And that's why everyone in these parts called it *calou ou cales, li voou, li vas.*'

That very afternoon, Cabassac and Julieta visited the mill themselves. It lay in ruins at the base of a deep mountain ravine. Alongside it ran the very cascade that had once provided that squat little hydraulic factory with all its energy. The waterfall tumbled from one boulder to the next, bursting into spume at one moment, then slipping – skein-like – in so much uninterrupted white water at the next. That afternoon, though, they'd approached the mill from the wrong side. They'd come down the narrow ravine on the opposite side of the mill itself through a high, overhanging stand of fir where spotlit beams of sunlight pierced the canopies to speckle the ground before them with a miraculous little flora of its own. Their quick, breath-bitten exchanges echoed – ricocheted – in approaching the cascade below. The torrent grew louder and louder until, finally, neither of them could hear the other but only the thud and hiss – thud and hiss – of the waters beating their way down that wild staircase of strewn boulders. In reaching the torrent itself, Cabassac felt Julieta tugging at his coat sleeve, laughing as she did. She was trying to tell him something against the roar of the cascade, but he heard nothing whatsoever as he watched her lips open, her teeth glitter, her cheeks contract to that same repeated message. Pointing at Cabassac, now, she shouted 'you' over that deafening tumult. 'You'll have to carry me,' he heard her say, 'carry me across the waters,' she said, laughing as she said it.

Tall as she was, Cabassac was even taller and wearing, that day, a pair of high rubber waterproof hiking boots. Of the two, he was far better equipped to make the delicate crossing. Coming to a series of broad, spray-lacquered boulders in tight succession – clearly a fording point in its own time – Cabassac took Julieta in his arms and carried her across in several well-calculated leaps. With Julieta's arms wrapped about his neck and her long, slender legs projecting well past his propped elbows, Cabassac was astonished by her lightness. Astonished, too, by that rich, resinous scent that seemed to issue out of every pore of her being, intoxicating Cabassac as he brought her, still laughing, onto the opposite side of that frothing, turbulent cascade. There, though, he couldn't bring himself to release her, deliver her – as intended – to the very foot of that ruined water mill. Her black hair gone steel blue in that bright light, the hair itself slapping against Cabassac's cheeks in a wind that rushed though the narrow ravine, he felt himself grow increasingly powerless. He felt that vast yet ultimately flimsy superstructure – that scaffold of constraints, displacements, sublimations: all the aspects by which he'd always recognized himself – collapsing under the weight of Julieta's weightless gaze. He felt, in its place, another power, far older, simpler, emerge. It jammed every nerve, tendon, corpuscle of his body. As if acting on its own volition, it brought Cabassac's lips flat against hers, found him – to his own astonishment – feeding on those lips with the points of his teeth, drawing them in, under, pulling her by whatever means he had into his undertow, that deep, tidal extraction, tugging just then at her belt, the tongue of her buckle slipping loosely past its last notches as the two of them dropped, now, against the pine needle floor and found themselves – naked to the thighs – in a narrow puddle of plummeting sunlight. Cabassac, now, began caressing every fold and contour of Julieta's body, while Julieta – lying elongated, an arm behind her head and a single knee raised, almost languorously, against the light – received Cabassac with a near-perfect, near-unflinching passivity. She let him happen, let him fondle and

70

sip. Suck and gnaw. Let him penetrate, now, forcing his passage in blunt, vibratory thrusts, swelling concentric to her very depths, wild to her calm, wet to the scarce lubricity of her bunched muscles, eyes wide – agape – to the long, fanned arabesque of her loosely interlocking black lashes. Julieta neither encouraged nor demurred. Like a spectator, a *voyeuse*, an interested third party to that whole remote enactment, she pleasured in Cabassac's repeated thrusts but only, in a sense, as an absentee. Alongside that cascade, deaf to Cabassac's heated suspirations, hearing nothing but the thud and hiss, thud and hiss of those wild, tumultuous white waters, Julieta fell into a deep rapture of her own, there, just there, where a water mill was once heard to say:

I tumble down, you tumble down;
I go under, you go under.

Three weeks later, with the wind blowing wild in the courtyard beyond and the shutters banging flat against their swing hooks, Julieta awoke vomiting. She sat up immediately, wiped the vomit from her lips with the tip of her bedsheet, and broke into a smile such as Cabassac, lying alongside her, had never seen. He gazed across in amazement. Since that afternoon at the water mill, they'd come to share the same room, the same

71

bed, even – in Julieta's case – the same striped flannel pajamas. More passive than complicitous, however, Julieta had maintained that ambivalent distance – that curious erotic remove – just as she had at the cascade three weeks earlier. This reserve seemed to excite Cabassac all the more. Two, three, four times a night, he'd enter into that narrow set of flexed tendons in a wild, exhilarating attempt to penetrate the very depths of that distance, reach, at last, the cryptic source of Julieta's inherent enigma. Close as he'd come, though, he came no closer. Not until that very morning, three weeks later, did he feel – suddenly, unexpectedly – that distance dissolve. Julieta's innate reserve – that curious erotic remove – had altogether vanished in a single, luminous moment. Wiping vomit, now, from the corner of her mouth and smiling as she'd never smiled before, she gazed not past, not through, but – for the very first time – directly into the heart of Cabassac's being.

'Isn't it just possible?' she asked excitedly. But before Cabassac could even answer, she climbed out of bed and vanished into the bathroom next door. When she returned, moments later, smelling of honeysuckle and dressed in a fresh pair of pajamas, she held – delicately as a plucked flower – a thermometer between two fingers. 'I mean, given the lapse of time,' she continued, 'couldn't it just possibly have happened?'

72

'Of course,' he said. 'Of course, it's possible,' he repeated, feeling at the same moment a pang of resentment, even jealousy, rush through him.

'Oh, don't you think so, Philippe?' she repeated, laying the thermometer down, now, on the night table and hugging Cabassac about the neck. In the process, she'd just called him – for the first time – by his very own name.

'Of course, of course,' he whispered as reassuringly as he could, smelling that resin – that rich, natural unguent – invade his senses as Julieta, now, came to rub her cheek against his shoulder and neck, to run her long arms about the full breadth of his waist. 'Oh tell me. Tell me it's true, Philippe,' she pleaded, wanting to hear out loud – in so many words – what her own body asserted, now, with each passing minute.

So he told her. Told her over and over what she already knew; what, instinctively, every covert signal of her being faultlessly declared. If, in that very moment, Julieta felt her own wildest aspirations confirmed, Cabassac felt his, quite suddenly, volatilize. He realized, just then, that he'd never come to possess Julieta entirely. He'd never enter into that idyllic state of total complicity which excluded – by its very nature – all others. He'd never penetrate to the very depths of her being and return, holding her, her alone: her – at last – entirely his. Now, he realized, they'd no longer be a couple but a threesome. Already, in fact, that tiny bundle of miniature organs had begun rooting, feeding, extracting its vital fluids from the very flesh Cabassac venerated with an all-consummate passion. As object of his own monopolistic cult, Julieta alone constituted the only 'other.' Within his own heart, there wasn't room for yet a third. A child in her own right, Julieta could be the only recipient, Cabassac felt, of an adoration that was every bit as protective – even paternal – as it was unabashedly lustful.

'Bless you,' she breathed over Cabassac's shoulders, her lips moving, now, over his neck. 'Bless you, bless you, Philippe,' she murmured as Cabassac, his eyes clamped shut, rose turgid, now, into a relationship he could in no way have anticipated, let alone chosen.

From that morning forth, it was spring in Julieta's heart. Spring quite literally, for the cherry trees in Provence had just burst into a plethora of stout phosphorescent bouquets. Spring, too, as she felt that wizened little creature swell within her viscera, wrap itself against those taut, elastic walls with an assertiveness quite its own. Never had Julieta pleasured so much in her own body. Never had she stood as now naked before a full-length mirror, letting her arms run supple to her very fingertips, and her fingertips fold podded about that nascent globe. She'd stare and stare, for never as now had she found so much to admire in her own reflection. Before that very mirror, she'd rub her body down, lacquering it in almond oil to a single, glistening piece of workmanship. With long forceful strokes down her long, slender legs and round, molding movements about her breasts and swelling belly, she'd become both the model and craftsman of her own free-standing creation. She took half a step backwards, now, and – palms flush against her tall, oily hips – beamed into her own reflection.

It was spring, both in the air beyond – luminous, effervescent – and in the dark involuted chamber of Julieta's womb. At the very same time, she'd begun writing her dissertation, a lexicon of sorts, covering each and every term (in each and every one of its dialectical variations) for the now defunct cultivation of silkworms. Hadn't Julieta been introduced to that magical world, Cabassac recalled, by that circle of women who'd taken her in, and, for several weeks running, fed and sheltered and fondled her long body in a cocoonery somewhere near Valensole? The cultivation of silkworms, it so happens, also occurred in springtime. It was a fact of spring. Over a brief but intense six-week cycle, the silkworm was 'reared' from its egg and brought to pupation. Spring was not only in the air and in the coursing of Julieta's own organic fluids but in her day-to-day research, as well. Throughout her entire pregnancy, she remained a devoted scholar. Furthermore, the cultivation of silkworms was – by its very nature – an exclusively female occupation. It required a woman's nurturing patience and meticulous care. The subject alone, she quickly discovered, perfectly befitted her own inner state at that exact time. With one spring lying as if concentric within another, she sat at her little oakwood table, and – fountain pen in hand – began scratching out the first pages of her treatise.

With both Julieta and Cabassac heavily involved in their own research, they had little time to spare. Their own marriage, in fact, a cursory affair with only two mandatory witnesses in attendance, lasted no longer than the ceremony itself and two, three, rounds of pastis in the neighboring café. That night, celebrating in their own fashion, they made love tenderly, cautiously, and called one another, with mocking humor, *monsieur* and *madame*. Next morning, though, each was hard at work, once again. Chasing down a lost human activity by the bias of its own virtually lost grammar gave Julieta a particular satisfaction. She felt she was rescuing, saving, that lost economy from extinction. Felt that here, too, she was involved with the business of life. She began, then, at the beginning: with the eggs, that is: with that spawn of infinitesimal pearl-like seeds (*la grana*) which women poured into little sachets (*estoupouns*) that they'd sewn for the very occasion. Wearing those sachets underneath the warm folds of their skirts or snug between their corseted breasts, they'd incubate those nascent silkworms on nothing more nor less than the heat of their own bodies. Soon, they'd bring the eggs to hatch, but only after the first tender shoots of the white mulberry (*l'amorié blanc*) had sprouted: once the nourishment, that is, for these writhing little offspring could be assured.

For ten days running, then, women actually served as agents of gestation for these silkworms-to-be. As mothers of many, the women would then deposit the freshly hatched larvae in nurseries – kindergartens of sorts – that they'd have meticulously prepared in advance. Temperate, airy, well-lit, these cocooneries (*magnanarié*) became the silkworms' abode, now, as they passed through four successive moltings in as many weeks. Growing from delicate little caterpillars no more than a millimeter long to pale, voracious creatures a full sixty times that length, the silkworms required continuous nursing. And nursing they received. Laid out on wooden trays (*levadous*) that were stacked one on top of another like beds of a bunk bed, they'd feed on ever-increasing quantities of mulberry leaves. If at first they'd only nibble on the tenderest shoots, after the fourth molting they'd ravish as many leaves as an uninterrupted succession of wagonloads – stacked hay-high – could provide. The roar of their

77

munching during that period (*la granda frèso*) has sometimes been compared to a torrential downpour in the midst of a dry deciduous forest.

Reading every source available, interviewing anyone who might still retain some memory of that twilight economy, Julieta went about compiling her lexicon. Comparing one regional variant with another, 'controlling' the value of each specific term, she accumulated an invaluable amount of ethnolinguistic data as spring progressed. By June, she reached in her writing that critical moment in the life of silkworms wherein the fully developed larva stopped eating altogether, and – discharging every impurity from their entrails – grew perfectly translucent. Grew 'clear as a fully ripened white grape,' as one entomologist once remarked. At that very time began the *encabanage*: the moment in which the silkworms, as if on some magical signal, rose into their brushwood uprights (*enramas*) and began spinning their cocoons. Rotating their heads continuously so that a thin, spittlelike secretion would run free of a pair of matching glands located on either side of their thorax, these creatures would each spin over a kilometer of precious, opalescent fiber in less than three uninterrupted days of labor. Nothing stopped them, either. Nothing aside from unwanted noises. A single thunderclap, for instance, could break the thread, bring their spinning to an end, destroy a whole season's harvest. When a thunderstorm was seen approaching, women – in preparation – would gather, begin ringing bells – goat bells, sheep bells – or beating, gently at first, against shovels, frying pans, cauldrons in an attempt to prepare their little nurslings for the far more invasive sounds of the thunderstorm itself. They'd increase the volume of those cacophonous medleys with each passing minute. In response, the silkworms wove all the faster, and their thread, as a result, went unbroken throughout the ensuing thunderstorm.

In writing about silkworms, Julieta had evidently found the perfect metaphor for her own incipient condition. She'd come to explore therein a whole hidden universe of gestation, especially as those little spinners approached term and wrapped themselves more and more snugly within the rich silken walls of their immaculate shell cases. Readied themselves for the miracle of transformation into so many fluttering butterflies.

'This is the part, though, I can't write,' she confessed to Cabassac one afternoon. 'Can't admit to.' The two of them had been working side by side at a long table before a pair of open window-doors. 'The moment, that is, they collected the cocoons. That's the part I can't bring myself to express.'

'The stifling, you mean?'

'Yes, the stifling, the *estoufage*,' she replied. 'When they take the cocoons down off their brushwood ladders and steam them so that the butterflies won't escape. Won't burst through their shells, destroying in the process all that carefully spun thread.'

'But the thread's everything,' Cabassac retorted.

Very gently, Julieta shook her head. Her hair seemed to quiver like a kind of liquid. 'No,' she said, 'the thread's nothing in itself. It's only there to protect – envelop – the life to come.'

'For the women, though, the thread was everything,' Cabassac insisted. 'For generations of *magnanairé*, those women whose only income throughout the year came from that month and a half of uninterrupted nursing, fostering, cultivating, it was everything. As their only source of pocket money, it represented – no matter how small, how slight – autonomy itself. It represented some little life of their own.'

'It didn't, though, for the butterflies,' Julieta murmured as she went to stand by the tall open window-doors. Framed against the already dense foliage in the courtyard beyond, her hands lying cupped about her belly, Julieta spoke as if to herself alone:

'No, not for those stifled little butterflies,' she repeated. 'No, not for them. Not in the least.' As she said this, she couldn't help but picture those quiescent little creatures writhing in their shell cases as the steam rose –

lethal – through the sealed boxes, there where they'd been terminally consigned.

Had Julieta, that very instant, foreseen her own fate? Foreseen a night, only a few weeks later, of violent abdominal contractions, followed by a flush of hot, sticky, irrepressible body fluids running down the inner flank of either thigh? Foreseen the death of her own chrysalid? She'd been told by her doctor, a full month earlier, that the fetus was 'poorly positioned,' but, with sufficient care and attention on the mother's part, it would come to term without any undue complications. Now, that very same doctor, alerted at three in the morning, stood over Julieta's bed, shaking his head. It was already too late. The ambulance that took her to the local hospital needn't have rushed, needn't have used its siren, needn't have come to the curb of the emergency entrance with such a hollow show of bravura. Julieta had already lost her most precious possession.

After a series of obstetrical examinations a week later, she was told that she could never bear children; that an irreparable malformation of her uterus would keep her from ever giving birth. In response, Julieta insisted on second, third opinions; went through a series of examinations in yet other hospitals; waited without appointments for hours at a time in one doctor's waiting room after another. Every examination, however, only came to confirm the first. For all intents and purposes, Julieta was deemed barren. 'Barren,' the word alone echoed through her being like a death sentence. 'Barren, barren,' she kept repeating, feeling as she did that she'd never confer upon an offspring, now, the kind of legitimacy that she herself had been denied. Far worse, though, she'd never fill that immense emptiness she had always known by mothering her own child, generating the kind of parental love and tenderness that she herself had always yearned for.

'Barren,' she whispered as the two of them walked, one afternoon, across Cabassac's abandoned cherry orchards. Cabassac himself couldn't recall which of those orchards, grainfields, oak woods still – in fact – belonged to his own estate and which had already been sold off in that steady attrition: that annual sale of one parcel after another to meet his own albeit modest needs. Through the years, that estate had considerably dwindled. Now, as they came down through the unhoed, unpruned, untreated orchards – last year's cherries still dangling rotten from their rust-red stems – it occurred to Cabassac, only two weeks after Julieta's miscarriage, that she, too, was fading. Slipping away. That his whole world, in fact, was falling apart.

'I've decided to stop,' she declared suddenly. 'To

abandon the whole thing altogether,' she said as the two of them walked along.

'Abandon what, Julieta?' He had his arm wrapped loosely about her shoulders, but felt that he was holding on to someone who was no longer entirely 'there,' not even to the slight pressure that emanated from his fingertips.

'Abandon my studies, my research,' she said in a murmur, more to herself, finally, than to Cabassac. 'Everything I've been working on for the past months. None of it means anything any more,' she said out of that distance into which she seemed to have drifted. Eyes to the ground, she clutched in the tips of her fingers a tiny bouquet of wild thyme that she'd just picked. 'Dead words, dead phrases,' she went on, 'all those futile attempts to awaken a totally dead world. No, none of that interests me any longer,' she went on sullenly, bringing the little bouquet, now, flush against her torso like some kind of compress. Her voice had gone thin, distant, inaccessible. 'All the dead, all the descriptions of those poor dead creatures who chased bees, once, over a hilltop or banged on shovels, cauldrons, empty kettles to keep their silkworms spinning through a thunderstorm. All that has lost all meaning, now. All meaning whatsoever.'

Cabassac could remember when words – those 'little bits of reality,' she'd once called them – had meant everything to Julieta. When the acquisition of a specific term had allowed her to constitute a geography of sorts; when the preservation of those nearly extinct vocables had given her a sense – no matter how tenuous – of place, belonging, rootedness. Through language alone, hadn't she begun constructing a sonorous home of her own? Out of so many patiently collected phrases, the fragile outlines of a lost heritage? Now, she'd let go. Words, phrases, the endless entries she'd made in a lexicon of her own – yes, that vanished world of the *magnanairé* which she'd reconstituted – had volatilized. Now, she realized, that home she'd always hoped for would never happen. Nothing could shelter her, now, from the emptiness she felt, as vacuous as that sack that hung – a gutted fruit – from her own innards.

As the two of them reached the base of the hillside, Cabassac remembered the first time they'd walked together, heading to his car by the Avignon ramparts. He remembered noticing that millisecond's hesitation between her step and his; that infinitesimal increment of reluctance which had defined her space, her autonomy, her separate self, from the very start. It had immediately drawn, baffled, magnetized Cabassac, for it represented, in his eyes, distance itself: that depth in which all beautiful things resided. Even when they'd first made love by the waterfall, she'd maintained that interval, that tiny increment of inaccessibility. It wasn't until the morning, three weeks later, in announcing her pregnancy, that that interval had suddenly vanished, that distance dissolved. Turning towards him, Julieta's gaze had penetrated his with all its heart. Boundlessly grateful for what she could only consider life's greatest benediction, she'd at last yielded. Cabassac, taken by surprise and instantaneously resentful of that stranger, that third party, already ensconced in Julieta's womb, had failed to recognize such a benediction. Had failed to receive, that very day, Julieta's radiant gaze. Now, that gaze, that radiance, that boundless gratitude, had vanished forever. As they walked along, that afternoon, her voice reached him as if across some insuperable chasm. Even with his arm draped loosely about Julieta's shoulders, Cabassac knew that he was holding on to little more, now, than a stray spirit, a disincarnated creature.

'Dead words, dead phrases,' she went on. 'All the particles – the dead, grammatical particles – of that dead world,' she continued as the two of them came down out of the terraced orchards and headed toward Cabassac's broad, ramshackle farmhouse. As they did, Cabassac noted how she'd begun rubbing the brittle little spines of the thyme she'd picked over the flat, perfectly flat surface of her belly. She rubbed and rubbed until nothing was left but a blunt little stub. He held on to her, now, even closer. Close as he did,

85

though, he had to admit that he felt he was holding, tighter and tighter, on to no one, no one at all.

That very week, Cabassac came to accept full responsibility for Julieta's miscarriage. He did so out of a growing sense of the irreparable harm he'd unwittingly caused. Hadn't he received the news of her pregnancy with immediate misgiving? Thought of it as a veritable misfortune? Hadn't he wanted Julieta exclusively for himself and himself alone, and resented – from the very outset – that 'intruder,' as he called it? Only now had he come to realize how all this ill will, no matter how indirectly, might have affected that tiny fetus, deeply cradled in the folds of her womb. He convinced himself that he had crippled it forever and, so doing, crippled Julieta as well, depriving her of her very own double. Julieta, furthermore, had learned that the blighted fetus was female, a little girl, a little Julieta of her own. How, Cabassac wondered, could he have loved one without loving the other? How? he kept asking himself. His question stabbed at his inner self like a merciless little hand weapon that had taken on an autonomy of its own.

Julieta, in the meanwhile, strayed further and further. If, at first, she helped Tanto Mirèio in her vegetable garden – planting and hoeing, potting and repotting, ending the day smelling every bit as green as the plants she tended – she took, more and more, to the woods beyond. There, other roots, other foliage awaited her. She began reaching backwards, roaming into any space that might possibly have anteceded her own. For Julieta, nowhere was far enough. It was as if her only possible future lay, now, in those netherworlds, those antediluvian residues that she found for herself in the scrub oak directly behind that broad, dilapidated farmhouse. There, in that moorland, she came to discover an order that preceded her own: the flora and fauna of a nature yet untamed, undomesticated, obedient to nothing more nor less than the unalterable cycle of the seasons themselves. There, there was no iron to stave, prop, train the grapevine, nor baling wire to enclose so much free-running game. No plowshares, either, for furrowing the earth or insecticides for empoisoning the air. In the *garrigue*, a natural environment still provided for the nourishment, protection, and reproduction of its species. Self-regulating, it needed nothing, either – least of all, man – to thrive in the very midst of its own intricate biosphere.

'Oh, Magalie,' Tanto Mirèio would bemoan, 'you've left me once again.' For she loved having this young woman she'd mistaken for her very own daughter as a helping hand in her garden. She loved the way Julieta – tall, lanky, loose-limbed – stooped to regulate the flow of water through the narrow irrigation ditches that ran

87

trickling between rows of lettuce, pepper, zucchini. 'Like a boy, just like a beautiful, beautiful boy,' Tanto Mirèio marveled. She loved, too, how Julieta, humming to herself, would walk toward the house, balancing on each hip two sagging straw baskets full of fresh garden produce.

But Julieta, now, was elsewhere. 'Oh, Magalie, Magalie, how many times are you going to leave me?' Tanto Mirèio asked. No one knew exactly where Julieta went on that raised, calcareous moorland, nor how, in fact, she spent her time except by whatever wild fruit or mushrooms she'd return with at day's end. Sometimes, too, she'd come back with a wood thrush cupped in the palms of her hands that – undoubtedly – she'd caught between the collapsed slabs of a fall-trap that she'd set for such purposes. A hunter-gatherer, Julieta had entered into a paleolithic world entirely her own. Silent, perfectly remote, she'd go on staring at the dead little bird she kept cupped between the palms of her hands. It lay there inanimate as a pebble.

Inanimate, too, she lay alongside Cabassac each night, perfectly limp. Like a body drained of everything but its image, its odors, its own most outward manifestations, she lay as if embalmed – exhibited – upon the raised table of their bed. There was no question, now, of lovemaking, of intercourse. To the contrary, Cabassac held Julieta – or, rather, Julieta's wraith – as one might hold a cloud or the running outlines of some wind-driven shadow. With immense tenderness, he drew this beautiful absentee flush against him, ran his hands through the glossy mass of her hair, and whispered – whispered in that nearly extinct language that both of them had shared – the earth-worn, earth-weathered expressions of his own inextinguishable adoration.

Then, one night, holding her against him as he would every night she'd given herself if not to his body at least to his breath, his whispers, he felt the fever. He felt every pore of her body break into perspiration as – all night – she whimpered in her sleep, letting out tiny, brief, truncated cries. The fever marked the beginning of the end. From that night forth, it only climbed, the perspiration only increased as her halting little cries became more and more frequent. More and more anguished. Julieta, thin by nature, began losing weight, now, to an altogether alarming degree. Within a matter of weeks, her cheeks had grown hollow and her long, lovely fingers spindle-thin. Her gaze, in turn, lost all its natural luster and her complexion grew increasingly wan, pallid, as if her body were being bleached from within. Despite the evident gravity of her condition, she refused to see a doctor. She refused, in fact, any medical attention whatsoever. Cabassac noticed how she'd lean more and more against a wall for support or hold on to a door handle a moment longer than she might. Even if she still made an occasional foray into her beloved *garrigue*, she'd return all the weaker a few hours later with a pocketful of hazelnuts or a little bunch of Michaelmas daisies as if blooming out of her fist. Even these brief excursions, though, grew rarer and rarer. Clearly, she was fading fast and there was nothing and no one, now, to impede the ineluctable. Nothing and no one she'd entrust herself to. Cabassac speculated that she was suffering from a cancer of the uterus. What else could consume her so quickly? He pleaded with her, of course. Begged her night after night as – soaked head to foot – she clung to him not as a lover but as, perhaps, already a memory, a fast-fading memory.

'We have to see someone,' he pleaded.

Shaking her head, she murmured: 'there's no one to see.'

'A specialist. We could go to Marseilles the first thing in the morning, Julieta, and see a specialist.'

'No,' she said, 'there aren't any specialists, don't you understand? For things like this, there's no one at all,' she declared flatly, impassively. There wasn't the least trace of self-commiseration in her voice, either; only pure, unmitigated resignation. For Julieta, her life had already ended. It had ended with the realization that it would have no sequel, no prolongation. That she had lost the power, now, to generate past herself life's veritable, ongoing dimension.

'You won't forget, though, will you?' she murmured unexpectedly. They were lying, now, eyes to the ceiling in the first light of dawn.

'Forget what, Julieta?'

'That morning,' she whispered, her voice barely audible from the rustle of leaves in the outlying courtyard.

'Which morning, Julieta?' Cabassac asked, suddenly insistent, holding on to anything he could: any scrap, any tiny residual, seemingly inconsequential remark she might make. Cabassac knew that he was about to lose her, and collected – like relics – every word he could against that fast-approaching eventuality.

'That morning,' she said, 'when the wind blew. When it blew just like this, and I woke up with the wind blowing, and tasted, for the very first time, vomit on my lips. You won't forget that morning, will you?'

'No,' he vowed, 'I never will.'

'The shutters, too, were banging just like this, I remember. Banging just like now as the vomit rose clear to my lips. I've never tasted anything so sweet, never in my life.'

Cabassac took her by the hand. 'No, my Julieta,' he promised her as solemnly as he'd promised anything in his life. 'No, I assure you, I never shall.'

'So sweet,' she murmured. 'So terribly sweet,' she uttered, her eyes half closed and her voice thinning, now, into nearly nothing at all.

Three nights later, Julieta rolled over against Cabassac's heavyset frame, and froze. Her fingernails dug into his shoulders and her legs twisted inexorably about his. She didn't cling, that very instant, so much as mineralize. It took Cabassac a long and terrifying moment, indeed, to extricate himself from her final clutch. Fingertip by fingertip, limb by limb, he came to detach himself, nonetheless, from the one person on earth who'd bound him – inextricably – to life. And, as he did, as Cabassac worked free of Julieta's frozen form, his love – simultaneously – etherealized. From that moment forth, Cabassac entered into an order of his own making. Julieta dead would now become Julieta transfigured; the chilled corpse, from that very instant, the figure out of which, hallucinatory, his own blazing icon would emerge.

It was Tanto Mirèio who prepared Julieta for inhumation, dressing her in ivory-white linen and speckling her hair with those gaudy little plastic roses as she had when Julieta first arrived in Cabassac's nearly deserted farmhouse. 'Magalie, my Magalie,' she bemoaned as she placed an artificial tulip, now, between Julieta's crossed hands. The blossom stood in violent contrast to Julieta's deeply sunken cheeks and the long, gothic outline of her wasted frame.

'Now you've left me forever, haven't you? Flesh of

my flesh, heart of my heart, now there's no one, no one, no one at all,' Tanto Mirèio intoned well into the night. Her quivering little voice echoed throughout the rooms of that vast, dilapidated farmhouse, hollowing out its each and every volume even hollower – emptier – than ever before.

Next morning, Cabassac discovered his poor bereaved aunt had prepared the entire house for mourning, as well. She'd done so in the most traditional Provençal manner. She'd draped all the mirrors in the house with black crêpe and detached the pendulum from the tall grandfather clock in the hallway. According to ancient custom, these measures allowed the spirits of those recently deceased to rise all the more readily, unhampered by either their own reflection or any gratuitous reminder of human time.

Several days later, Cabassac would discover yet a third funerary custom that Tanto Mirèio had observed. Wandering into the *garrigue* one afternoon, following the very paths Julieta must have taken onto that raised, windy heath, he came across a row of broken-down beehives, hammered out of scrap bits of board and lined with scrap bits of tin sheeting. The beehives themselves probably hadn't served for nearly half a century. In fact, Cabassac could just recall his grandfather, a gauze mask over his face, fumigating those boxes one after another. Now, in passing, he saw how his aunt had covered each of them in yet more of that same funerary crêpe. Saw how the black crêpe itself quivered in the wind against those derelict hovels.

Standing there, staring down at them, Cabassac felt that his life had already happened. Had already rushed under. Even the very moment, now, seemed part of an all-consummate, all-devouring past. From that instant forth, he realized, he'd have to invent yet a second life. Staring downwards, watching how the crêpe beat against the flanks of those abandoned boxes, his thoughts could only rise. Reach upwards.

III

'Because I have something wonderful, perfectly marvelous, to tell you,' Julieta had assured him in a dream he'd had two years after her death. That dream, those words, had not merely intrigued but obsessed him ever since. One can even say, in fact, that since the night of Julieta's dream declaration, he'd thought of little else and had gone about preparing – months in advance – what had come to be his dream season: the season, this is, of truffles. For only in those richly induced states, provoked by the consumption of that mysterious tuber, would he enter into contact, once again, with the object of his bereavement. Cabassac, in fact, spent the spring, summer, and early autumn of that year as if those very seasons had no other reason for existing aside from the covert production of so much subterranean fungi. For him, all of nature, now, had become little more than a pretext for the germination of those singular mushrooms.

His calendar, suddenly, became theirs. Beginning in

April, he knew that the already desiccated truffle would have begun releasing its ascospores from innumerable little spore cases. And these, in turn, transported at random by wind, insects, birds, and mammals, would soon burrow and sprout into white filaments: mycelia, as they're called. With good fortune, these mycelia in their underground migrations ultimately encountered the tiny rootlets of some host plant and, so doing, initiated symbiosis. In this very union – the virtually accidental encounter between the swimming threads of the fungus and those, say, of some holm oak – the truffle is born. Somewhere between April and June, the tuber – in the form of a minuscule bubble or blister – germinates. Within this reciprocal relationship, the truffle comes to supply water, nitrogen, mineral salts to the tree in exchange for sugars and proteins that the truffle couldn't otherwise have provided for itself.

Cabassac realized that this wedding of filaments is one of nature's miracles. Theophrastus had considered the truffle the work of lightning and rain, and Porphyry that of the very gods themselves. It inspired deference, respect, awe. Was it merely coincidental, Cabassac wondered, that it took the truffle exactly nine months to reach maturity? Before reaching maturity, though, it had to surmount endless obstacles, satisfy endless conditions. The truffle needed a calcareous soil, for instance, but not excessively so; rain at certain specific moments of the year, but not others; a terrain lying at a pitched gradient for maximal rain runoff but only within strict geomorphic limits; frost in which to ripen come winter, but only for a brief, prescribed period. Indeed, there was virtually no condition favorable to the truffle's growth that didn't contain – like some kind of codicil – its own inherent counter-condition.

Throughout the spring of that third year, Cabassac remained vigilant. Already, he realized, the truffle was entering the first in a long series of potentially annihilating trials. If the truffle itself needed a certain amount of heat and humidity in which to grow, too much rainfall in late spring could drown its still tender, groping rootlets. Equally, a late-spring freeze could nip the minuscule tuber long before it reached maturity. Consequently, Cabassac found himself tapping the barometer, staring out windows and observing – with ever-increasing attentiveness – the movement of clouds, the least trembling of leaves in the great plane tree in his courtyard. If all the elements were willing – if the heavens, that is, were favorable to the earth and allowed the dream tuber to reach maturity come November – Cabassac knew that he'd learn, at long last, what Julieta had meant when she said that she had something 'wonderful, perfectly marvelous' to tell him.

That spring, Cabassac even scrutinized the manner in which magpies built their nests. An old Provençal adage claimed that the lower the nest, the colder the forth-coming winter would be. In fact, Cabassac read all nature, now, as omen, prophecy. Nothing in the air above didn't foretell, months in advance, what he'd be unearthing out of the impacted ground just beneath. As spring advanced, indeed, Cabassac did little more than anticipate his dream life for that coming winter. He went on teaching, lecturing, but only in a kind of trance: his intellectual life had begun turning into something vaporous, unreal, at exactly the same moment that the preparation for those truffle-induced 'visitations,' as he called them, grew into the sole remaining reality in his life.

As spring progressed, he received repeated warnings from the Rector at the Université d'Avignon. He was being reprimanded for the quality of his lectures ('vague,' 'inconclusive,' 'contradictory,' according to student re-ports) and, even worse, for far too frequently failing to appear for the lectures at all. If Cabassac even bothered to read these warnings, he ignored them completely. Stea-dily, now, his classes emptied out. Each week, fewer and fewer students appeared in that once privileged, intellec-tually animated environment he'd created. Cabassac was the last to notice this disaffection; last to notice anything, now, but the way the wind moved through the paulownia in the auditorium's skylight window. Or, occasionally, how the moon – in that very same window – had acquired an all-auspicious halo.

Fortunately for Cabassac, the school year ended before his increasingly irresponsible behavior could have caused his dismissal. Without knowing it, he'd been granted a reprieve. Oblivious of his profession, his scholarship, of the very world around him, Cabassac grew inordinately happy whenever a light rain shower touched the parched earth toward the very end of spring. These rainfalls, he knew, would quench the thirst of the still minuscule tuber just long enough to bring the truffle to that diacritical moment in its development: that of the double *Damos*. The double *Damos* occurred between *Nosto-Damo de l'Assoumcioun* on August 15th and *Nosto-Damo de la Nativeta* on September 8th. During this period an abundant rain had to fall for it is just then that the truffle undergoes a period of exponential growth. With an overall rainfall, say, of five or six centimeters at this time, the truffle can grow between a hundred and a thousand times its size in a matter of days. It is just at this moment that the truffle breaks free of its symbiotic relationship with its host, and becomes an autonomous growth unto itself.

Cabassac waited. Waited while the air grew heavier and heavier as mid-August approached and each afternoon a thunderhead – seemingly the same – amassed in the east. Ever darker, more voluminous, its immense, upswept structure quivered with tiny veins of lightning. It wasn't until August 20th, however, that Cabassac actually heard the lightning, and not until the 23rd that a few fat drops of stillborn rain splattered against the parched leaves of the great plane tree in his courtyard.

It was Tanto Mirèio, in fact, who – five nights later – predicted the thunderstorm's veritable arrival. She brought candlesticks and a pair of kerosene lamps to the dining table, where the two of them – since Julieta's death – had begun taking their meals together. Their loss had brought them together; brought them, each evening, into a tiny circle of complicity. Now as Tanto Mirèio laid those candlesticks and kerosene lamps onto the table, she declared: 'You won't finish your *pistou*, I can assure you, before the electricity blows out.' Then added, almost gleefully, 'You'll see. You'll see what a wonderful fortune-teller I am.'

And, sure enough, halfway through that thick, steaming basil-based porridge – far more solid than liquid – a lightning bolt fell within the very courtyard no more than ten meters away. And, as it did, a fuse blew in the fuse box and plunged the entire house into total darkness.

'There,' Tanto Mirèio cackled, joyous with her powers to predict such things. 'There, there,' she howled with delight as she went about the table, a match cupped within the tiny transparent bowl of her fingers, lighting one candle after another, then the wicks of those battered brass tall-sleeved oil lamps. Doing so, her face filled from under, grew radiant in a tight network of wrinkles. 'You see, you see,' she cried out jubilantly.

By now, lightning bolts were falling in tight succession so that the end of one bolt and the beginning of the next seemed as if welded one to another. The walls shimmered white as tin while the floor trembled from under with the thunder's steady percussion. 'You see, you see,' Tanto Mirèio went on while Cabassac, corkscrew in hand, twisted open a bottle of his oldest, fullest-bodied Vacqueyras. For the lightning storm had brought with it a kind of release. Brought a certain light-headed elation into the dark room and corridors of that somber ramshackle farmhouse. Pouring out two goblets, he raised his own in the direction of his aunt. It was Tanto Mirèio, however, who proffered the toast.

'To Magalie,' she proposed. 'To our own beloved Magalie.'

'Yes,' Cabassac agreed. 'To Magalie.'

'Wherever she is. Wherever she happens to be tending, this very moment, some beautiful garden.'

'Yes, wherever,' Cabassac echoed, his wineglass wobbling with reflected lightning as he brought it, that very instant, to his lips.

That night, lying in bed, Cabassac not only heard the rain striking the hollow pink roof tiles just overhead but the sudden, sharp, percussive ping of hailstones. Ever since

103

childhood, he'd been told that the truffle, the *fru de glaço*, had always been considered the fruit of that atmospheric phenomenon. He had no idea himself how the ancients had first come to associate one with the other: that icy white projectile falling out of the heavens with that black, buried, hermetic tuber underneath. Nevertheless, that association had always proven to be true, especially if those hailstones fell as they did that very night: between, that is, the two *Damos*. Altogether, they couldn't have been more propitious.

As often the case, that late-summer thunderstorm was followed by an unabated blast of mistral. Often called the 'mud-eater,' it dried, even crackled the surface of the earth. Within a matter of days, the topsoil grew as parched as a desert floor. Cabassac read this as a kind of signal. A geomorphic clue. Given the extent of the truffle's inordinate growth rate immediately following that late-summer thunderstorm, its rapid swelling blistered the surface of the earth a full twenty, thirty, even forty centimeters overhead. It left what is called a *pèd-de-poulo* or chicken-claw imprint upon the earth's surface. Cabassac knew exactly what to do at such times. Putting a handful of barley seeds in his pocket, he went out onto those abandoned terraces of his, following the line between the oak woods on one side and the dead almond, cherry, and apricot orchards on the other. Whenever he came upon one of those *pèd-de-*

poulo, he dropped barley seed into its very center, then moved on to the next.

That morning, he spotted and marked well over a dozen such sites. Within weeks, he knew, the early-autumn rains would have effaced those chicken-claw imprints, choked their tiny crevices with running silt. By then, though, those barley seeds would have sprouted, leaving – each time – a thin little pennant of rose-gold spikelets, trembling in the wind. Infallibly, the pennants would indicate the presence, just beneath, of some incipient truffle.

It was only September, however. There remained nearly two months before *Sant Crespin*, October 25th, when the white truffle was said to turn gray, and a full two and a half months before *Santo Magarido*, November 16th, when, with the first ground frosts, the gray truffle finally turned black. Then and only then could that mysterious fruit begin to be harvested. Meanwhile, Cabassac had to contend – once again – with teaching, lecturing, offering tutorial services to his advanced students. Week after week, he drove into Avignon, keeping an eye as he went on the sky, on cloud formations, on the least variation in wind flow. Nothing else mattered now but those atmospheric variables which, all autumn, would come to determine his dream life that winter. It's not that Cabassac didn't dream of his dead wife throughout the entire year, but only in momentary flashes, brief snippets: a glance, here; arms wrapped snugly about her knees, there; a phrase tattering in midair, there again. Come winter, though, it was another matter. Come those winter nights, he'd ingest a dark, savorous tuber and enter into what he himself called that *dispousicioun*. Dreaming entire episodes – whole glossy sequences that unreeled like film strip and lasted, it seemed, like little eternities – he'd enter, once again, into communication with his beloved Julieta.

He parked his car, as always, along the ramparts and walked to the university as if driven by nothing more than some deepseated automatism. Moving to the lectern to address an ever-decreasing number of students, he began murmuring, repeating himself, or, losing track of his own moot argument, trailing off into a series of vaporous non sequiturs. Often, too, he fell silent. At such times, an attentive student would have noticed that each time this occurred, Cabassac would be staring: staring into the very last vacant row of that auditorium. He stared as if magnetized to the contours of a particular seat, as if the seat itself were charged with a plethora of ionized particles, and – drawn by those very particles – he could do nothing, utterly nothing, but stare and stare.

Come October, Cabassac was placed on probation. He received a long, reprimanding letter from the Rector in which he was warned that his recent conduct would no longer be tolerated. Appended to the letter was a list of the dates on which he'd failed to appear for his own lecture series, and extracts from an ever-growing number of student complaints. It's not altogether certain, however, that Cabassac bothered to open this letter, let alone read it. In fact, it's not altogether certain that Cabassac bothered to open any of his incoming correspondence any longer. Not only letters but invoices went ignored. Second, even third notices for overdue water, electricity, and telephone bills went unanswered. Philippe Cabassac, though, was 'elsewhere.' Indeed, as the truffle season grew nearer, he seemed to have abandoned the preoccupations of the present altogether for the bountiful promises of a rapidly approaching future. With only that future in mind, he gave himself more and more to a whole series of preparations. Keeping an eye on the sprouting barley he'd planted in those *pèd-de-poulo*, checking out patches of scorched earth that gave every indication of being productive, he'd already entered the realm of the eventual. The physical world that immediately surrounded Cabassac – his walls, his rooms, his house – had long since turned into something transparent, immaterial. Indeed, only the earth beyond, only those impending ground frosts that would bring the first black tubers to maturity, held any meaning, now, whatsoever. As a man with a long-awaited rendezvous, Cabassac could think of nothing else.

107

One night in early November, his house was plunged into total darkness. In default of payment, his electricity had been cut. For Cabassac, curiously enough, this didn't seem to matter. He and Tanto Mirèio ate dinner together by candlelight as they had the night of the lightning storm, two months earlier, then took their tisanes by an open fire in the living room. Anyone entering that living room at that very moment would have been struck by the setting itself. Cabassac and his aunt were plunged not merely into a household without electricity, but into a traditional Provençal decor such as hadn't existed for over half a century. They sat silently by an open fire or played *belote* at a tiny card table – the crack of cards adding its timbre to that of the hissing cinders – absorbed in their own thoughts and as far removed from the bleaching incandescence of lightbulbs as any two people could possibly get. Listening to themselves, their own inner thoughts, or, perhaps, the hissing of those very cinders, they'd appear to anyone entering the living room at that given instant as the relics of a civilization that had long since vanished.

Sometimes, too, Cabassac thumbed through the pages of an almanac quite by himself. A relic of its own, the almanac was the only publication he consulted, now. It not only contained such vital information as the phases of the moon, the conjunction of planets, and the exact hour of eclipses, but the time-worn, time-tested adages of an entire agrarian culture. He was in the midst of reading one

such adage touching on a snow-bearing midwinter wind –
la rodo – when the telephone rang. Reluctantly, Cabassac
rose and took the call in the next room.

'Philippe?' he heard a distant, vaguely familiar voice
ask over the receiver. 'Is that you, Philippe?'

He assured her it was.

'Really you, after all these years?' she asked in a voice
that was far too familiar, too intimate, given the nature
of their relationship. 'Promise me, though,' she pleaded
in a whisper, her mouth – quite evidently – close to the
receiver. 'Promise me you'll tell no one, no one whatsoever, that I'm calling. Please, for my sake, promise.'

And so he did. And just as soon as he did – had sworn,
that is, their conversation to secrecy – Magalie asked if
they could meet. 'Anywhere, anywhere you say, but
soon. Right now, if you can possibly make it. Tonight,
tomorrow morning, but soon,' she pleaded in that
heated whisper of hers.

Cabassac suggested that they meet the following night
at the Café Fin de Siècle in Cavaillon. The café, a candy
box of mirrors, rococo moldings, and frescoes as if
floating in oval medallions overhead, seemed the perfect
setting for such an encounter. The following night,
thoroughly puzzled, he arrived there only a moment
before she did. And, as she did, as she came through the
café's elegant glass doorway, Cabassac was struck by the
resemblance. Tall, sinuous, with a glistening tuft of dark

109

hair and long, somewhat pendulous black eyes, she did indeed resemble Julieta.

Taking her seat, she cupped her hands about Cabassac's and spoke in that same, heated whisper: 'You didn't tell her, did you?'

Cabassac shook his head.

'Not a word?'

'Not a word.'

'How is she, anyway?' she asked rather hurriedly, looking over one shoulder as she did.

'She misses you. She misses you terribly.'

Returning her gaze, now, to stare at Cabassac and cupping her hands about his even more insistently than before, she confessed: 'Philippe, I'm in trouble. Lots of trouble, and it's something I don't want her – or anyone else, for that matter – to hear about, do you understand?'

'Trouble? What kind of trouble?'

Turning her head about once again, she sought out a waiter and ordered herself a whiskey – a double whiskey – while Cabassac ordered a *café exprès*. 'What kind of trouble?' he repeated.

'Something happened,' she told him as soon as she'd taken a deep sip of her whiskey. Doing so, she shook her head, sending her hair into a sudden, glossy wheel – a glistening disk – before settling into her account of what, exactly, it was all about. She mentioned a party she'd been at several months earlier in downtown

Quebec. 'A pretty wild party – I have to admit – but no more than most.' It had lasted all night long, apparently. 'Sure, I was smashed, but so was everybody else,' she explained, glancing over one shoulder. 'Everybody, I can assure you,' she insisted.

'What happened exactly?'

'Driving home, I hit a kid, a little kid on her way to school,' she explained, taking another long sip of her whiskey. 'I never saw her. But I heard her as her body hit the fender and went flying. Heard the quick little scream she made as she flew off to one side,' she told him, cupping Cabassac's hands, now, tighter and tighter. 'Philippe, I need your help, don't you understand? I need your help badly,' she whispered in a single, sustained rush. The smell of whiskey struck him across the tiny space that separated, now, their two faces.

Cabassac could already foresee the rest. Could predict – point after point – the remainder of his cousin's story. How she'd been arrested after the accident by the Quebec police and been immediately booked for manslaughter, hit-and-run driving under the influence of both narcotics and alcohol, and – most likely – insult to a public officer. How, in turn, she'd been jailed, then released a few days later on bail, and – once released – had fled not only the city and the province of Quebec itself but the country altogether in a wild attempt to save her own dissolute life.

111

'Please, Philippe,' she urged, running her thumbs over his knuckles and into the narrows at the base of one finger after the next. 'I'll do anything, anything you wish, but help, help me, Philippe, I beg of you,' she said, bringing her face, now, close against his.

Gazing straight into that very face, Cabassac felt obliged to admit that – feature for feature, characteristic for characteristic – Magalie and Julieta might well have been sisters if not twins. Tanto Mirèio, in fact, hadn't been altogether mistaken. The same broad, dolorous eyes and long, elegant nose; the mouth as if lifted into a near-permanent look of expectation; and yes, even the cleft chin could only remind him – and grievously – of his own beloved wife. In fact, that very moment, grinding her thumbs into the deepest recesses of his palms and bringing her forehead flush against his, she not only looked like Julieta but emitted, through a pungent screen of whiskey, a faint resinous scent – a coniferous signal – much like Julieta's. Cabassac thrilled to the resemblance. As her black lacquered hair slipped forward, now, and stung his cheeks with a tiny electrical discharge, he felt the current it emitted sizzle through his entire system. Reach to his very depths. There was nothing about Magalie that didn't look, smell, feel like Julieta. In fact, as the two of them sat there in that dark, richly paneled café, their foreheads locked and the thumbs of one grinding impetuously into the palms

112

of the other, all Cabassac could hear was water. Was rushing water. Was the frothy, white, irrepressible pour of that mountain torrent where, four years earlier, he'd first come to possess Julieta: where their very voices had lost themselves to the thud and hiss – thud and hiss – of all that thrashing turbulence.

'Well, will you? Will you help, Philippe?' she asked, kept asking, working her thumbnails, now, deep into the soft shoal of his hands. 'Will you?' she insisted. But Cabassac, deaf from the sound of all that plummeting white water, hardly heard a single word Magalie said. Hardly heard anything, just then, but the thud and hiss – thud and hiss – of all that opulent plumage where even the sudden wild declarations of that distant afternoon got ground into the roar of an inexhaustible Alpine torrent.

'Well?' she asked, bringing her mouth up against his, now, so that Cabassac's lips actually quivered from the pressure that her words exerted. 'I'll do anything, anything you ask, anything you wish. Name it, Philippe, and it's yours.'

Had Cabassac been a bit more worldly, been a bit more versed in the ways and means of casual relationships, he would have led Magalie, then and there, to any one of the roadside hotels in the immediate area that catered to such situations. But Cabassac scarcely had the choice. Driven by a deep-seated, long-standing instinct, this middle-aged bachelor invited Magalie, that very moment, to return to the one place on earth that he knew: his ramshackle farmhouse in the hills. Without an instant's hesitation, she accepted, ran a hand over his thigh, and planted a prolonged kiss over his lips. She agreed, furthermore, that once they'd entered the house, she'd be perfectly silent, do nothing to disturb her sleeping mother, and leave – the next morning – long before her mother had awoken. She insisted, though, on having one more whiskey – a 'nightcap,' she called it – before the two of them finally left the café and walked arm in arm to Cabassac's parked car in the square beyond. There, just as soon as the car doors had slammed shut, Magalie shoved herself up against Cabassac, ran a long slender hand between his legs, and virtually blew into his teeth: 'Promise me, Philippe. Promise me this very moment.'

Cabassac could only nod, deaf as he was to virtually everything but that plummeting white water that beat against his eardrums. 'Out loud,' she insisted. 'Promise me out loud,' she said, her skirt pulled, now, about her waist, and her knees planted solidly on either side of Cabassac's heavyset frame.

So promise her he did. Over the roar of those irrepressible waters, he promised that he'd do everything within his power to raise whatever money she needed.

'Whatever?'

'Whatever,' he reiterated, and felt, in the same instant, her slender body slip over his.

'Now,' she said, biting at the rim of Cabassac's ear, 'how about driving me back to that house of yours, huh?'

Once inside Cabassac's great dilapidated farmhouse, though; once the two of them had pulled, tugged, yanked one another's clothing off, and tumbled onto that wide, tightly sprung bed of his; once, at last, Cabassac had brought Magalie under and driven himself into her very depths, the sound of those deafening waters abruptly ceased; the roar of the cascade – resuscitated only an hour earlier – fell suddenly mute. Now, all he could hear was the quick little cries of his cousin below, above, counterposed against him, as she exulted – over and over – in his own desultory attempts to penetrate not merely a body but to the very heart of a beloved being. Soon enough, though, Cabassac had to admit the utter failure of this simulated experience. Aside from the relentless lash and ripple of his cousin's body working tirelessly against his, he was holding on to nothing more, now, than an empty semblance, a sham replica. To Magalie's repeated orgasms, Cabassac could only respond with disheartened indifference.

Some time later, that night, Cabassac must have fallen asleep. Some time later, as well, Magalie must have made her way downstairs and begun routing about for alcohol in the kitchen cabinets. What awoke him, though, wasn't Magalie herself but the sound of glass, glassware, crashing against the kitchen floor. In rummaging about a house without electricity, she'd inevitably let something fall. Cabassac, in response, held his breath. He listened to the throb of his own heartbeat while his eyes probed the dark walls of his room in search of some familiar object, some slight reflection. What he feared most, however, happened – happened ineluctably – a moment later.

'Who's there?' he heard his aunt cry out. 'Who's there?' she kept repeating as she shuffled, now, into the kitchen directly below. She'd be carrying, Cabassac realized, a flashlight as she came. Then, after a long moment's silence in which, Cabassac could only imagine, Tanto Mirèio had trained that flashlight upon every feature of her own daughter's face, she cried out: 'Who are you, anyway? What in God's name are you doing, breaking into someone's house? Who do you take yourself for?'

Cabassac heard Magalie attempting to explain herself. He heard the word 'mother' repeatedly. 'Don't you remember, it's me, it's Magalie, it's your own little girl.'

'Magalie?' Tanto Mirèio pealed.

'Yes, your own little Magalie,' she assured her. 'I've come all the way back from Canada, *maire*, just to see you, be with you, look after you.'

'Magalie?' she reiterated, incredulous.

'Yes, *maire*. It's me,' Magalie implored, moving now – Cabassac could only imagine – forward to embrace her very own mother. 'What's more, I've brought you a present. It's in my hotel room right now, but I'll bring it, ribbons and all, tomorrow morning. I promise, *ma maire*,' she uttered in wrapping her arms, now, about the shoulders of that stout little figure.

'Magalie? Magalie?' Tanto Mirèio queried, her voice gone suddenly soft, gentle, and – at the same time – perfectly remote, for the very name alone, it seemed, had set her mind to wander, her spirits to drift.

'Yes, yes,' her own daughter reassured her, tightening her grip about her mother's shoulders as she did. 'It's me. It's me, don't you remember?'

'But Magalie, my Magalie's in heaven,' the old lady protested. She was addressing no one, now, if not herself, raising her eyes – Cabassac could only imagine – toward the smoke-stained ceiling overhead. That's where she is,' Tanto Mirèio exclaimed, her voice gone perfectly calm, self-contained, serene. 'She's gardening, tending a little garden in some marvelous place of her own. That's where she is, my Magalie.' Fallen into a deep-seated trance, Tanto Mirèio intoned:

'Oh, who but a mother can recognize her very own.' As she said this, Magalie tightened her grip. Held to her mother all the harder.

'Oh, who but a mother, 'Cabassac kept hearing as he dressed hurriedly and rushed downstairs to separate the two of them, and lead this poor, delirious aunt of his back to her own quarters in a far wing of that dilapidated farmhouse. Magalie, in the meanwhile, stood aside, observed the whole spectacle as someone excluded, extraneous. She, now, had become the orphan. Throughout the slow, steady peregrination back to his aunt's bedroom, walking in a puddle of light that her flashlight cast against the broken floorboards, Tanto Mirèio didn't for an instant stop reiterating that same, inexhaustible refrain:

'Oh, who but a mother can recognize her very own. Her very own flesh and blood.'

Calculating the considerable sum of money it would take for Magalie to establish a new life for herself (he never for an instant believed her declared intentions to restitute the funds she'd already forfeited, hire a competent lawyer, and – after standing trial – prepare herself for not only a prison sentence but the payment of a sizable amount in liabilities), Cabassac telephoned the realtor. There was little else he could do. Next day, in the realtor's office, when he declared the amount he needed, the realtor whistled in amazement. The realtor wasn't displeased, either. He'd been purchasing parcels of Cabassac's estate for years, now: a few abandoned terraces, here; a swath of moorland, there; an outlying dependency – a dovecote, a silk cocoonery – yet there again. No, the realtor wasn't in the least bit displeased. He had already come to possess a better part of that vast property within a relatively short period of time. Curiously enough, though, he hadn't resold a single square meter of that once flourishing estate. What was he waiting for? Cabassac often asked himself. For all of it? For every last little patch of earth? For every door and door handle and rusting keyhole?

A day later, Cabassac and the realtor met at the notary's to sign the hastily prepared deed of sale, dense with conditions, correctives, amendments. It was already November, now, and Cabassac – dismayed by the hollow, duplicitous experience with his cousin – had his mind on other things. While the notary read out the immensely complex conditions of sale, Cabassac, all the while, stared through the window. Stared at a moon, floating over a hillside, three-quarters full. The window, a small, square-shaped peep-hole, was encased on every side by shelves of thick, archival record, bound in bone-white parchment and dating, in some instances, from the Renaissance. The moon, in the midst of all that impacted human testimony, seemed to float like a free agent, like some celestial emissary. Buoyant, aloof, it drifted free of so many centuries of dispute and litigation, of an endless succession of notarized deeds in which each and every scrap of earth had undergone sale and exchange, concession and preemption, the scraps themselves leased and divided, claimed and counter-claimed, redistributed – over and over – like cards in an unending cardgame that knew neither interruption nor conclusion. That afternoon, the moon in its swollen ellipse drew Cabassac well past the affairs at hand. It drew him past the droning intonations of the notary, reading out – clause after clause – the conditions under which such and such parcels of Cabassac's estate would be conceded that very day of that given year for such and such sums of money to the given name(s) of the realtor(s) in question. As to the sums themselves, he'd already stipulated that they be deposited in an account Magalie had just opened in a chic resort town along the Riviera.

Cabassac, his mind on the moon, signed the seventeen-page deed without having examined, let alone heard, a single one of its many intricate clauses. He might, in fact, have signed with his eyes still gazing at that celestial body, calculating as he did some extemporaneous figures of his own: how long it would take the moon, for instance, to turn and, in turning, provoke at this time of year the first serious ground frosts. For the moon, come November, heralded the truffle. Heralded, for Philippe Cabassac, his dream season.

He signed away his entire estate, in fact, without even knowing it. Without, perhaps, even caring. He was far too intent watching that lunar body swell, bringing – as it did – his Julieta ever closer for anything else, now, to matter.

IV

T hat winter, three years after Julieta's death, Philippe Cabassac spent long stretches of summer with his beloved. In dream after dream, they'd meet, embrace, and – talking in an animated rush – pass hours, sometimes days, in each other's company. Even if the dreams only lasted, in actual fact, a matter of minutes, they appeared as if suspended in a time frame entirely their own. In protracted sequences, the dreams went on and on as if they'd been immersed in a world elastic as honey, transparent as amber.

Once again, the dreams began in mid-November. Cabassac had managed to rout out a seventy-five-gram black truffle just a few days after the first ground frost had brought it to maturity. As always, he observed a three-day hiatus before dicing it into fat sections and consuming it with a runny omelette. He did so out of both tradition and superstition. It was a custom in Provence to let the truffle 'embalm' the eggs for those three days, the truffle hermetically sealed in a glass jar along with the eggs themselves. In regard to superstition, Cabassac – as a residual vestige, no doubt, of Christianity – held the trinity in unerring respect. He did everything in threes. He'd even fill his fountain pen three times: then, on a third fill, let three pendulous drops drip free of the gold nib. And so it was with the truffles. The trinity, at all costs, had to be respected.

Thus, with the first truffles, came the first suspended dreams. Came a series of apparitions that would unravel, all winter, like so many consecutive episodes in an unbroken drama. In preparation, Cabassac entered – once again – that little set of ceremonial gestures he'd established for himself. Having ingested the truffle in the running gold of its matrix, he'd sit by an open fire, drink a deep bowl of verbena, leaf absentmindedly through some scholarly treatise, and let himself be taken – bit by bit – into that all-auspicious state: that *dispousicioun*, as he himself liked to call it. Sitting there, he'd wait until the tall pendulum clock in the empty hallway struck nine. Then, at nine exactly, he'd retire. Upstairs under the low beamed ceiling of his bedroom, the bed, the double pillow, and starched sheets (meticulously folded on either side at the exact same oblique angle) all lay as if in preparation to receive not just himself but another.

And another, indeed, there'd be. No sooner had Cabassac slipped between those ceremonious sheets and begun reciting in a little litany of his own the last words Julieta had pronounced in the very last prolonged, truffle-induced dream he'd had the previous winter, than – in his falling asleep – she reappeared. She reappeared murmuring: 'I have something wonderful, perfectly marvelous, to tell you.' This time, however, she wasn't calling out to Cabassac across a distance. In fact, she could scarcely have been closer. 'What?' he begged her, 'what is it, my Julieta?' In way of response, she pulled his hand down below the line of her waist and pressed it against her lower abdomen. 'Feel it?' she whispered ardently. 'Do you? Do you?' she went on, wedging his hand against her belly all the more by pushing their two bodies together into a single, statuary mass. He felt, in fact, the very same, nearly imperceptible swelling that he had three years earlier, only more so. Only fuller, somewhat rounder, as if Julieta's pregnancy hadn't suffered interruption but had gone on developing, thriving. 'Isn't it marvelous, Philippe? Isn't it the most marvelous thing on earth?' she asked. And Cabassac, without a second's hesitation, responded: 'Yes, yes, my Julieta, yes, it certainly is.' For in the intervening three years, he'd come to make peace with his own conscience. Come to realize – in his heart of hearts – that he'd not only been witness but participant in life's greatest miracle. For here, in this invisible third, lay the only possible issue – over time – for the couple itself. Lay, indeed, its ultimate dimension.

'Come,' she whispered, 'let's go upstairs.'

'Can you, though?' Cabassac replied anxiously. 'What about the doctors? What did the doctors say?'

'Come,' she beckoned. 'Just be careful, that's all. That's all we need to worry about. Just go slowly,' she urged, leading Cabassac up the dark stairway by the hand and drawing him into the very bedroom – beneath the very rafters – where, in fact, he lay that very instant, dreaming that very dream. It was as if the dream had come to superimpose itself – like some blinding illumination – upon his all too disconsolate body.

'Slowly,' she repeated as he drew her slacks down about her ankles, then her underpants, and found himself feeding once again on that dark mollusk, that deep, seeping organism that had taken on – with pregnancy – an entirely new succulence of its own.

'Shh . . .' she whispered, lying back, now, onto the bed. 'Shh . . .' she repeated to remind Cabassac of her condition as he came free of his own clothes, now, and brought himself naked alongside her, feeling, as he did, the very tips of her fingers guiding him towards and under and into that very succulence without a single instant's hesitation.

'Shh . . .' she went on.

'Shh . . ., shh . . .' she kept saying throughout the night as the two of them made love as slowly, cautiously, painstakingly as two people could, enjoying, as they did, one ardent climax after another.

'Shh . . .' she kept reminding him.

'Shh . . .' she kept saying. All night, along with her gentle entreaties, Cabassac couldn't help but hear the waters of that distant Alpine waterfall grow louder and louder. Indeed, they fell louder that night than ever before.

The following week, it snowed. The snow in itself, Cabassac recognized, was something altogether favorable, for it kept the truffle snug under its protective cover. Furthermore, the snow discouraged predators. For not only truffles but boars, badgers, meadow mice, even those slow, voracious snails – the *Helix promatea* – were drawn by the truffle's suave, subterranean perfumes. The snow, then, kept the truffle not only from man but from every other form of mammal, bird, gastropod. After several days, though, Cabassac began tapping the glass of his barometer, consulting the thermometer, wondering when the snow would melt and the ground – once again – reappear, rife with those tiny, straw-like, tell-tale flies. But the temperature in those early days of December only fell and the moon only filled, more and more luminous, glacial, with each passing night.

'*Malan*,' he cursed between his teeth, staring out at the blank expanse before him. The moon virtually spotlit the double row of mulberry trees that lined the drive down to the country road below. '*Malan*,' he repeated, his violet eyes squinting into that lunar glare while he stirred a bowl of verbena that had lost all warmth whatsoever. That coming week, he knew, there'd be no balm, no cryptogamic potion to carry him – as on some mythological raft – to his beloved. No, nothing to bring him not only to Julieta, now, but Julieta doubled, compounded. What's more, in Cabassac's mind, there wasn't the slightest doubt: she could only be pregnant with a little girl. With, that is, a little Julieta of her own.

That night, he dreamt of them – both of them – but only in broken sections. Only in brief glimpses. Like bits of shattered mirror, these dreams – unprepared, unprovoked – left Cabassac feeling all the lonelier. They were neither coherent nor sequential. He awoke the next morning to hear Tanto Mirèio moving about downstairs, stoking the fire in the living room, her *pantoufles* shuffling across the soap-smooth flagstone slabs. This, in fact, is how he'd awaken, now, morning after morning. His life had turned into something totally mechanical, systematized. Aside from those stunning dream visitations, he'd entered into a rigid set of repeated gestures, movements, events, in which nothing – utterly nothing – could happen that hadn't happened already. Each day resembled the last, as did each meal, each page of some endlessly long pedantic dissertation. As for his teaching obligations, Cabassac hadn't so much dismissed them as forgotten them altogether. A registered letter from the Rector at the university – a final warning – had gone unopened, as had an ever-growing pile of utility bills. Quite clearly, Cabassac was 'elsewhere.' His dream life had come to represent the only vivid, meaningful moments, now, in his entire existence.

'*Malan*,' he went on cursing, staring out at that bleak landscape that had lain frozen, now, for two consecutive weeks. It wasn't until the outset of the third week, in fact, that the ice began thawing and little islands of brown earth began reappearing in the very midst of so much glazed, tenacious white. A southwind blew, now, transforming the ice into mud, and bringing with it a balmy midwinter reprieve. Once again, birds took to the fields and began pecking at whatever brittle little seeds they could find. In a matter of days, the ground had thawed sufficiently for Cabassac to whittle a fresh branch of Aleppo pine into a tiny whisk broom, and begin beating – once again – the bushes at the very edge of the oak woods.

This time, though, the truffles he unearthed (and they were plentiful) had already begun rotting from all the prolonged dampness. They were soft to the touch and rancid to the scent. He'd have to go on waiting, he realized, for the temperatures to drop and a fresh generation of truffles to ripen under the nurturing influence of a dry, deep, indispensable freeze.

It wasn't, in fact, until late December that those very conditions were met, and Cabassac managed to unroot a perfectly healthy, pungent, hundred-and-fifty-gram 'black diamond,' as they're occasionally called. Three nights later, he entered into that highly codified set of ceremonial gestures that led to his bedroom, his double bed, and – just before falling asleep – that exact, scene-by-scene recapitulation of his previous dream. Its on-going sequel ensued in a matter of minutes.

In his dream, that night, Julieta appeared very much as she had the previous time except that her belly had swollen considerably in the interim: had grown at least two, three months rounder. They lay – once again – in that very same bed but quietly, now, still perspiring from head to foot as if they'd been making love only moments earlier, as if Julieta had just uttered a last, soft, elongated 'shh . . .' by way of tender admonishment. They lay there, burrowed in one another's shoulders, until tiny pencils of sunlight broke through the cracks in the closed shutters and speckled their bedspread with a plethora of sharp little luminous points. It was Cabassac, finally, who worked himself free – free of that body with its rich, resinous scent – and reminded Julieta of her appointment, for that morning she had a rendezvous with the obstetrician. That morning, the two of them would drive – as they often had – into Avignon. This time, though, it wouldn't be for a lecture: for the propagation of that all but dead culture that they'd devoted themselves to, but – to the contrary – for a birth. Not for the examination of some subtle grammatical variant in a virtually extinct idiom, but in order to prepare for a living creature.

'Excellent, excellent,' Julieta's obstetrician declared that morning as he removed his stethoscope from his ears and looked up with a warm, reassuring gaze. 'This time,' he declared, 'everything's in place' (*bien placé*, as he put it), 'and there shouldn't be the least problem come term.' He led them gently, almost complicitously, to the door and added in parting:

'I'm proud of you, young lady. Most proud.'

For the rest of the morning they went shopping on the rue Joseph Vernet. Cabassac bought Julieta several full-size maternity dresses and a handprinted silk headscarf, speckled with stars. Then, celebrating so much good news with an act of extreme self-indulgence, they lunched together in the terraced gardens of the Hôtel la Mirande. Beginning with a chilled, astringent *gazpacho* served in shallow ceramic soup bowls, they went on to savor *daurade royale au fenouil* and sip at tall goblets of Bandol. Julieta, holding her goblet pronged between two slender fingers, sipped – as the beautiful water bird that she was – from its very rim. Under the glossy spill of her hair, her long lashes, nose and lips formed – with that wobbling globe – a luminous composition of its own. Cabassac gazed on in adoration.

131

'Is there anything else you'd like?' he asked her.

'Nothing,' she assured him, smiling to herself as she said it. 'Absolutely nothing. There's nothing on earth I could possibly want more than what I have this very moment,' she confided, incredulous at all the good fortune that had befallen her. Laying her goblet, now, back upon the tablecloth and staring into its shimmering, citrine depths, she couldn't stop shaking her head as she repeated over and over, 'Nothing, simply nothing, Philippe. Absolutely nothing on earth.'

For lack of payment, the water supply was cut a week later in that great dilapidated farmhouse. It didn't make the least difference to Cabassac, however, let alone Tanto Mirèio. They went about their daily lives – the one scouring the hillsides for those rare tubers, the other cooking, trundling firewood, stoking woodfires – as if nothing had happened. They simply began pumping water from the well in the courtyard, and hauling it into the farmhouse in black, splashing buckets.

Exactly two weeks later, the telephone line was cut off as well. There was no possible way that Cabassac could have known this, since no one – no one, that is, since Magalie's surprise call months earlier – any longer telephoned that estranged household. Inversely, there was no one Cabassac would have considered calling. No one he would have wished to speak to: not, at least, amongst the living.

Cabassac and his aunt had come free of modern conveniences, one after another, without feeling the least sense of loss. Scarcely noticing the difference, they'd begun living without electricity, telephone, or public water: without those services generally considered indispensable to modern life. For Philippe Cabassac, nothing could be considered indispensable, now, but the mushroom itself. But the black tuber. But the deep, munificent effluences of that subterranean fruit that, night after night, put him in such a state of pure receptivity.

Throughout February, Cabassac beat the grasses with ever-increasing fervor. He'd thrash at one ground-hugging patch of stonecrop after another in an attempt to flush one of those flies – those golden diptera – from its cache. As always, he approached an auspicious area with a low, early-morning or late-afternoon sun directly ahead of him. That way, he benefited from a maximal amount of cross-lighting while casting no shadow, allowing *lei mousco* no sign of his imminent approach until the very last instant. The flies, heavy with eggs, loathed being disturbed at this crucial period in their life cycle. Reluctantly, they sprang rather than flew from their perch; then, after several minutes, returned as if magnetized to those same fixated points. Cabassac, faithful to his superstitious habits, would wait for the fly to return three separate, totally distinct times before he dropped to his knees and began scooping up the earth immediately beneath. Sniffing the soil as he went, cupping it between the palms of his hands and inhaling deeply, he dug in the direction of that fungic ether: that volatile, saline, sulfurous perfume.

One buried thing for another, he kept telling himself as he dug, his violet eyes magnified by his heavy steel-rimmed spectacles. Yes, one dark mystery for another, he said as he felt his whole body thrill to his fingertips' first encounter with one of those globular black fruit. Yes, felt as he did the earth crumble too readily about its taut, vascular mass. For how, indeed, could he keep from thinking that, in touching one, he'd be touching the other? That some invisible current – sharp as lightning and subtle as dust – connected the two?

That February, truffles abounded. And so, of course, did Cabassac's dreams. In one after another, he followed Julieta's pregnancy on a near day-by-day basis, and became – so doing – not only a partner but an accomplice to that gathering mystery. He could even feel, with each passing dream, his own heart fill to that growing rotundity. Yes, swell to its swelling. The dreams, moreover, not only had an immense emotional impact on Cabassac's life but a practical one, as well. For there were any number of immediate considerations for which he and he alone held himself responsible. First, of course, there was the question of the nursery. Where would the baby sleep? The two of them discussed the various alternatives as they walked along the River Sorgue in a long, intensely bucolic dream that Cabassac had that month. Crossing a vaulted wrought-iron bridge, they could see themselves reflected in the smooth emerald sheath of the Sorgue's running current. Could see the long, flowing switches of the willows overhead wrap in reflection about the equally long bronze river weeds, just beneath. Leaning her head, now, against Cabassac's shoulder, she gazed lazily down at the waters, and whispered:

'With us, Philippe. Wouldn't it be wonderful if she slept with us? Yes, the three of us in the comfort of a warm, well-lit bedroom of our own. Wouldn't it, Philippe? Wouldn't it be wonderful?'

He drew her even closer so that her head burrowed into his neck, and the soft lacquered black of her hair – with its rich, resinous, combustive scent – lay pressed against his cheek. 'Yes,' he could only agree. 'It certainly would.'

It's difficult to say when exactly Philippe Cabassac crossed the line: when the immense wealth of his dream life came to invade and, finally, overcome the impoverishment of his day-to-day awakened existence. As the

135

latter slipped from his consciousness, he found himself more and more consumed – engulfed – by dreams. By dreams alone. Bit by bit, the barrier between his two worlds had vanished. He'd begun, for instance, making repairs about his house that he'd neglected for decades: replacing floor tiles or the worn wooden treads on the stairway, replastering the flue in the kitchen chimney. Consciously or not, Cabassac was getting ready. He was preparing his house for that beloved little family of his. In his last dreams, hadn't Julieta appeared nearly on the point of delivery, her belly enormous and her gaze gone languid, serene, blissfully remote? He'd have to work fast now, he realized. Have to turn that dilapidated farmhouse into something worthy of receiving those cherished creatures. He'd have to put everything in readiness in the very little time, now, that remained.

During those late-winter days, Cabassac seemed to move about his house in something of an animated daze, acting more out of compulsion – out of so many urgent, deep-seated signals – than conscious choice. Hammering here, reinforcing there, he gave every appearance of someone functioning without any forethought whatsoever, his violet eyes riveted – but like a sleepwalker's – on whatever task lay at hand. With each passing week, now, this condition grew more and more acute and Cabassac himself more and more estranged. By late February, he no longer lived *for* his dreams but *within* them. As Julieta approached term, for instance, he dreamt that the two of them discussed – in ever-growing detail – the practical aspects of caring for a newborn. In one of those dreams, Julieta was sorting out baby clothes, laying them in meticulous little piles across their immaculate white bedspread. From where Cabassac was standing, they looked more like pastries, like *galettes* neatly stacked in some *pâtissier*'s window. 'Bibs,' she murmured somewhat dreamily, 'there aren't enough bibs, Philippe.' She trailed a long, elegant index finger about the ruffled edges of one of those pastry piles as she spoke: 'Next time you're in Cavaillon, you might think of picking up a few more. Maybe three or four if you think of it.'

Sure enough, the next morning Cabassac drove into Cavaillon and not only purchased half a dozen bibs at the local *Prénatal* but chose from memory each and every item of baby clothing that he could recall from his previous night's dream. Yes, he picked out diapers, undershirts, terry-cloth jumpers, even several pairs of mittens that weren't much bigger than *petits fours* and every bit as pink.

'What a lucky little baby,' the shopgirl exclaimed. 'When is she expected?'

Bunched within a heavy winter duffel coat, Cabassac seemed little more, that morning, than the massive corporal underpinnings of his own wild, weightless, ebullient gaze. 'Any day, now,' he said in nearly a whisper. 'Yes, any day,' he repeated breathlessly, his eyes alighting nowhere but glancing, now, from stand to stand, shelf to shelf, with a kind of crazed excitement.

'Will your wife be having the baby in our newly renovated *clinique?*' the shopgirl asked.

But Cabassac never heard her. His eyes had been caught by a pale violet reflection that seemed to be darting from one glass cabinet to another. Thoroughly fascinated, he came to discover that every time he moved, so would the reflection. When he blinked, it blinked, as well. Turning away, now, he watched it vanish. And, in returning, saw it reappear – quick, flickering – in the very same instant that he reappeared himself. He went on toying with that ephemeral little specter for some time, enthralled by the life it led so very similar to his own.

'Is there anything else I can do for you, sir?' the shopgirl asked, thoroughly perplexed, now, by Cabassac's behavior. But Cabassac was far too preoccupied by those violet fires that kept darting across the glass cabinets, that morning, to hear the young woman's question, let alone answer it.

In Provence, spring arrives early. And that particular year it arrived even earlier than usual. Flowering almonds are its first, infallible sign. Their rosy petals seem to burst free of so much black, desiccated wood, bringing with them – at the very same moment – a host of honeybees. Simultaneously, the air grows charged with the rich, ammoniacal scent of the blossoms themselves. Only days later, shrub after shrub of forsythia breaks into incandescent fire, and – just after that – japonica, too, in a rich profusion of pink coral-like droplets. Nature at that very moment of the year reasserts itself and sends up – one after another – its unmistakable signals.

For Philippe Cabassac, however, this boded badly. It meant that soon, very soon, the truffle season would be coming to a close, and – along with it – that immediate access into the only world, now, that mattered: that of Julieta on the very point of childbirth. Weren't the rising temperatures ominous enough? And the sudden plethora of moths, midges, ground insects? Soon, Cabassac realized, the peach trees would be bursting into flower, as well. And, like nothing else, this would mark a definitive end to that bountiful dream sequence: what, for Cabassac, had come to replace life itself. Hadn't he heard, ever since childhood, that timeless adage:

> Peach trees in bloom,
> Truffler's doom.*

Beating the ground, now, with added fervor, tapping against each and every shrub that lay in any of those

* *Quand lo pesseguier es en flors / lo rabassier es en plors.*

loose, burnt-out circles of earth – supple as mattresses of freshly carded wool, as one truffler had put it – Cabassac might just as well have been knocking on a door. Begging entry as he did. Pleading, not for a dream but for the only meaningful, all-consummate experience that he had left. Tapping, he might just as well have been pounding, imploring the grasses – the very earth before him – for the one substantiating reality that remained.

'Come on, come on,' he murmured, 'let's see your wings, your little wings.' For the *mousco* had grown scarcer and scarcer and could readily be mistaken, now, for other recently hatched flies haunting the very same bushes. 'Come on,' Cabassac murmured between his teeth as the temperature, that morning, went on rising and the likelihood of finding yet another truffle, that season, grew less and less. 'Come on, give me a sign,' he begged, 'just one more flickering sign. That's all I'll need.'

In the past, Cabassac might have heard – far overhead – the whistling of sparrow hawks as they taught their young how to fly. Never would those predators be as gregarious as at that time of the year. He would have noticed, too, the winter wheat going green – emerald green – on the distant outlying plateaux. But Cabassac was far too engrossed with the task at hand to notice anything, now, but the thin, evanescent movement of so many winged insects, springing from one low-lying shrub to the next. Tapped, patted, cajoled, they represented the immensely reduced field – the ephemeral chessboard – of Cabassac's wedged vision. He had eyes, now, for nothing else.

Had Cabassac, in fact, still belonged to the world, still been involved with the cares and preoccupations of the living, he would have noticed – that morning – not merely the whistling sparrow hawks overhead and the winter wheat going green, but the arrival of several heavy-duty earthmoving bulldozers along the very edge of what was once his property. Those stout, ungainly machines, indeed, had already begun breaking ground. Leveling the first outlying terraces, uprooting the dead wood that stood in their way, they maneuvered in one direction, then its opposite, reducing, as they went, the contours of that laddered earth to a single prescribed gradient. Clearly, the ground itself had undergone 'reappraisal' and lost, in the process, its agrarian status. A soil that had nurtured the roots of olive and almond orchards for millennia was being prepared, in a matter of days, for a future far different from anything it had ever known.

Had Cabassac still belonged to the world, to the cares and preoccupations of the living, he would have seen them. Would have heard them, at least: their steady, monotonous, gear-grinding ruminations. Heard their repeated roar forwards and their slack, relapsing hiss backwards. Cabassac, though, had his mind on flies.

Had his eyes riveted on the low-lying shrubs in which so much ephemera – thin as straw and sudden as eyelashes – might spring unexpectedly. Weren't these the keys, the golden keys – *lei claus d'aur*, as Cabassac called them – that led, by the bias of the underlying truffle, to the bountiful, swollen body of his beloved? No, nothing else mattered. Even more, nothing else even entered Cabassac's mind but what lay on the far side of sleep: on the opposite side of the proverbial mirror. He'd crossed the critical line sometime earlier, and begun wandering over the folds of an earth that only served, henceforth, as entry.

Had he bothered to open his mail over the past few months, he might – in extremis – have been recalled to the world of the living. Might have awakened to the fact that he had lost his job, his income, and that his house – without water, electricity, telephone – had fallen into total desuetude. Worse, far worse, he would have discovered a series of eviction notices – dry, succinct, irrevocable – advising him that he had only so many months, then so many weeks, then so many days to quit the premises altogether. For that winter, in a state of total distraction, he'd signed away his entire estate. At the notary's that morning he'd been far too preoccupied by the moon floating weightlessly in a small peephole window to consider anything but the moon's movement, its trajectory, its hidden portent. In a precipitate attempt to generate enough money to help Magalie reconstitute her life – perhaps even her identity – he'd signed whatever papers he was handed as he gazed and gazed at the moon beyond. For the moon, that morning, offered Philippe Cabassac every promise of an abundant truffle harvest within the immediate days to come. That, though, was months earlier.

Now, approaching the very end of the season, beating the grasses for the furtive trace of some evanescent *mousco*, Cabassac came upon the last black truffle of the year. He'd waited until a fly (heavy with eggs undoubtedly) had returned to its perched station three successive times, then – at that very spot – had dug a full forty centimeters straight down. The earth itself grew more and more pungent as he went. *Too* pungent, he thought to himself. And, sure enough, when he finally unearthed this last tuber of the year, its ripeness – he immediately detected – bordered on putrescence. It was several days past maturity. Held up to his nostrils, its scent, indeed, was overwhelming. Far more animal than vegetable, it smelt – in turn – of musk, sperm, fuming meats.

Waiting, now, the prescribed three days while the truffle embalmed a hermetically sealed jar full of freshly hatched farm eggs, Cabassac kept himself busy housepainting. He painted their bedroom, an adjoining pantry, and a long-abandoned storage space that he was

143

converting into a dressing room for Julieta. He worked faster and faster, now, as spring advanced, as the acrid scent of blossoming almonds blew through those empty rooms, bringing along with it a host of slow, somnolent honeybees. Breathlessly, now, Cabassac covered wall after wall in lemon yellow, the overhead plaster moldings in rich viridian, working uninterruptedly from one meal to the next. What with the windows wide open, he might have heard – just beyond – the bulldozers moving closer and closer with each successive day. Leveling the ground as they went, plowing up those scorched earthen circles in which Cabassac had routed out his truffles since childhood, they'd come within a few hundred meters, now, of the farmhouse itself. Within days, they'd be demolishing stables and dovecotes, chicken coops and rabbit hutches, all the dependencies that surrounded that long-coveted, steadily preempted farmhouse which had been sold by Cabassac months earlier for a certain amount, and purchased – days after – by a speculator for an amount far greater. According to the recently granted building permit – duly posted in the local town hall – the new owners of that farmhouse and all the outlying estate were given full permission to turn the former into a clubhouse and the latter into a rambling eighteen-hole, obstacle-free golf course. They'd be calling it, the permit read, 'Le Golf des Anciens Domaines (Club Privé).'

144

Cabassac, however, was far too preoccupied tracing a trim border about the edge of a bathroom wall to take the least notice. Heedless of the fact that he was painting, decorating, preparing a house that was no longer his, that he'd been truffling on property that he'd relinquished months earlier, he squinted down a razor-thin alignment and assured himself of its exactitude. Cabassac, indeed, was far too engrossed, far too removed, now, to consider anything but the task at hand. Furthermore, it was already three days, now, since he'd routed out his last truffle. Late in the afternoon of that third day, Philippe Cabassac began thinking of the dinner he had yet to prepare.

It would be Cabassac's last dream. He knew this, of course, and went about its preparation with more fastidiousness than ever before. Dicing the somewhat overly ripened truffle into perfect little rounds, he poured the rounds into three freshly battered eggs, and – stirring them together – let them fry no more than a minute on a highly preheated frying pan. He then ate this *brouiado de rabasso* while it was still hot, pressing it against the roof of his mouth with the point of his tongue. At the very same time, Tanto Mirèio sipped at her habitual vegetable broth: a plate that she far preferred. In fact, when Cabassac offered her a portion of those perfumed eggs, she turned him down with a wave of her hand.

'Don't you think I have enough memories already?' she asked lightheartedly. Together, though, they shared heavy slabs of country bread, slices of moon-white goat cheese, and glasses of dark, earth-dark, *vin ordinaire* from the local wine cooperative.

Within a matter of minutes, Cabassac began feeling that irrepressible sense of well-being as the knots in his nervous system unloosened and a kind of balm flooded every cell in his body. That night, indeed, he could scarcely wait for the pendulum clock in his hallway to strike nine before closing his book and climbing – candle in hand – to that freshly painted yellow bedroom of theirs. Yes, candlelight lapping against those glossy walls, the whole bedroom would glow, that night, like a single, incandescent yolk: the very color, Cabassac thought, of life's first substantiating nutrients.

Slipping between his coarse bedsheets, now, he let a hip pivot his entire mass into place, anchoring his body in position as it did. Firm to his very toes, he closed his eyes, now, and entered that litany of his own making. He recapitulated for the very last time his past dreams in chronological order, lingering especially on that luncheon they'd had in Avignon only weeks earlier. Within a matter of minutes, still murmuring to himself, he'd have fallen asleep. This time, though, his new dream erupted out of all sequence. Broke chronology. It raced forward three, four, five episodes, abandoning altogether those somewhat bucolic visions in which the two of them had discussed, in detail, each and every material consideration in regard to that fast-approaching birth. Now, quite suddenly, Julieta appeared perfectly massive, seated in a tall rattan armchair. Her bare feet firmly planted on the red floor tiles, she sat – stock still – in a flowing white nightdress. The nightdress covered her long, Junoesque frame, billowing frothy, nebulous, about her swollen midsection. Tanto Mirèio, hovering to one side then the other, was hard at work. She was in the process, just then, of removing those plastic flowers she'd once stuck into Julieta's hair, belt, buttonholes, behind each of Julieta's naked ears. She was withdrawing the long plastic stems of those funerary blossoms in evident preparation for the birth to come.

'Heart of my heart, flesh of my flesh, you can't fool a mother. For only a mother,' she reiterated, 'really knows. Only a mother, finally, can recognize her very, very own.'

Cabassac watched Julieta wrap a long, graceful arm about Tanto Mirèio's diminutive shoulders as the old lady plucked the very last of those plastic flowers from the black puddle of Julieta's hair. Then, stepping back, the old lady – her hands clasped together – surveyed the young woman like a painter her most accomplished painting. 'There,' she said. 'That's better, much better,' she murmured as, gnomelike, she gazed at Julieta sitting bolt upright in that tall rattan armchair. 'Much, much better,' she continued. 'That's the way it should have been from the very start.'

Cabassac observed the drama before him like a perfect spectator. Unlike every other dream he'd ever had of Julieta, this time he wasn't free to enter: partake, that is, in the dream sequence itself. Cabassac could only acquiesce. For there in that flickering interior lay a world of women: of two women, exactly. One of them, seated majestic as some kind of high archaic priestess, was on the verge of delivery. The other – half as tall and nearly three times as old – was preparing to assist. Every few minutes, indeed, Julieta's mouth opened – opened wide – as if to holler. Nothing, however, came forth. Clearly, she'd already entered labor. As the dream progressed, her mouth broke open – with ever-increasing frequency – into a near-perfect O-shaped orifice. Her holler, though, remained mute, immensely silent.

It was Tanto Mirèio, measuring the interval between each of Julieta's contractions, who saw that the moment was fast approaching. Hovering close, leaning her faded peasant's smock over Julieta's immaculate nightdress – the one smelling of cellars and fried onions and the other, perhaps, of the first inadvertent squirts of human milk – Tanto Mirèio began whispering an endless string of encouragements into Julieta's ear. Julieta, for her part, went on opening and closing her mouth, faster and faster, wider and wider, as the labor intensified. At a given instant, Tanto Mirèio must have realized that the delivery, now, was close at hand. Tugging at the cotton straps of Julieta's nightdress, she managed to pull it free in a series of quick, frenetic gestures. Drawing from one side then another, she yanked it up over Julieta's tall, glistening frame.

Cabassac could scarcely believe what he saw. Julieta, throning naked now in her armchair, had the very same svelte shoulders as ever – drawn at perfect right angles to her arms – but both her breasts and belly had grown utterly immense. Her firm, pubescent, near boylike breasts had swollen into two sagging glands, fat as grapefruit. As for her nipples, never bigger than pencil erasers, they, too, had turned thick, tumescent. They pointed like tight little nozzles, one in one direction, one in the other.

The words 'barbarous beauty' came rushing into Cabassac's mind, now, as he watched Tanto Mirèio kneel to the stone floor and spread Julieta's legs out before her. Yes, 'barbarous,' he thought, observing the vulva that seeped profusely, now, between the thick, convoluted folds of the labia, while the labia themselves pulsated scarlet under so much unrelenting stress. 'Barbarous,' he insisted, this inaugural moment to all human existence which had no precedent whatsoever: only *suites*, sequels, only – with good fortune – the emergence of spirit out of flesh, mystery out of meat, all the

149

buoyant impalpables of the heart bursting forth from that broken sack. It was exactly this, now, that trickled forth in the form of amniotic fluid, running down the inner flanks of Julieta's thighs, lacquering them slick as marble while Tanto Mirèio – serving as self-appointed midwife – came to cover Julieta's entire vulva with her plump, calloused hand, caressing, assuaging, pacifying as she went. Yes, 'barbarous beauty,' he kept repeating as Tanto Mirèio, having massaged Julieta's entire pubic section with astonishing deftness, pulled Julieta – at the given moment – by the calves downward and drew her knees fully apart with a slap on the inner side of each thigh, all with an equally astonishing authority. For it was Tanto Mirèio, crouched in her stained peasant's smock, who first saw it. Saw the crown of that fetal head breaking through. Under the pressure, now, of each successive, relentless contraction – scarcely seconds separating one from the next – saw that tiny crown spread Julieta's vulva fully apart like some perfectly elastic, endlessly expansive membrane. And now, not only saw it but brought her rough, peasant, ungloved hands forth to receive – with a vehement half-turn – this infant, this long-awaited, long-adored infant into the world at long last.

Only then, in that very second, did Julieta let out a howl. The howl itself must have arisen as much from relief – from sheer, unmitigated relief – as it had from pain. If, however, it began in a grimace drawn across the lines of Julieta's exhausted, heart-shaped face, it ended in a soft, relapsing, beatific smile. For Julieta had just been granted everything she'd most deeply desired in life.

The same howl that had heralded the baby's arrival awoke Cabassac, in the same instant, from this, his very last dream. He awoke ecstatic. For he, too, had just achieved plenitude. Julieta's joy could only be – indissociably – his own. He awakened, now, to a house fully prepared, ready to receive this family of his. Nothing had been overlooked, nothing had been forgotten – he realized – but flowers. Yes, flowers. And now that the peach trees were in bloom, marking the end of the truffle season (hadn't he recalled since childhood that age-old couplet *Peach trees in bloom, / Truffler's doom*?), he dressed as quickly as he could, took his pruning shears, and went out into the first flowering peach orchards. There, he began clipping, squeezing the icy pink peach blossoms free of their branches. Returning to the house time after time with brimming armfuls, he managed to fill not only the entry, the dining room, the stairway itself with bowl after bowl of those very blossoms but the rooms overhead: the pantry, bathroom, and – finally – the freshly prepared bedroom-cum-nursery itself.

Cabassac was upstairs when it happened. He was in one of those recently painted rooms, delighting in the scent of those flowers, when a small detachment of police officers entered the hallway below and began investing the house, two at a time. Finding no one on the ground floor, the *brigadier* in charge was the first to take to the stairway, warrant in hand. For he'd come to evacuate the house in favor of its new owners, and place Cabassac under arrest for having ignored three successive eviction notices. Cabassac, though, was busy with his flowers. So busy he probably never even heard the *brigadier*, followed by his small contingent, enter the freshly painted bedroom-cum-nursery. Cabassac was undoubtedly fussing with his pink blossoms, giving them some kind of radial arrangement – loosening, separating, juxtaposing one branch with another – when they entered. At that very moment, tears of pure, unmitigated joy were running down his cheeks just as the *brigadier* began reading out the charges set forth in the arrest warrant. Cabassac never heard him. Never heard anything henceforth but the great, fluffy, pink resonance that seemed to emanate, now, from those thick bouquets. For the blossoms themselves – that very instant – had begun resounding. Begun roaring like a wild surf in Philippe Cabassac's ears. And there was simply nothing else he could hear, henceforth, but that. Nothing whatsoever, now, but the roar of those icy pink blossoms, reverberating, over and over, within his eardrums.

A NOTE ON THE AUTHOR

Gustaf Sobin has lived for thirty-five years in Provence. He is a poet and has written two previous novels, *Venus Blue* and *Dark Mirrors*.

A NOTE ON THE TYPE

The text of this book is set in Berling roman. A modern face designed by K. E. Forsberg between 1951–58. In spite of its youth it does carry the characteristics of an old face. The serifs are inclined and blunt, and the g has a straight ear.